Eli Lundy Huggins

Winona

a Dakota legend and other poems

Eli Lundy Huggins

Winona
a Dakota legend and other poems

ISBN/EAN: 9783337391485

Printed in Europe, USA, Canada, Australia, Japan

Cover: Foto ©Andreas Hilbeck / pixelio.de

More available books at **www.hansebooks.com**

WINONA

A DAKOTA LEGEND

AND OTHER POEMS

BY

CAPTAIN E. L. HUGGINS
2d Cavalry U. S. Army

G. P. PUTNAM'S SONS

NEW YORK   LONDON
27 West Twenty-third St.   27 King William St., Strand

Knickerbocker Press

1890

The Knickerbocker Press, New York
Electrotyped, Printed, and Bound by
G. P. Putnam's Sons

CONTENTS.

———

WINONA : A DAKOTA LEGEND

WINONA : A DAKOTA LEGEND.

PROEM.

HOW changed, fair Minnetonka, is thy face
   Since first I saw thee in thy pristine grace.
Electric lights fantastically glow,
Swarming like fire-flies on the shores where long,
Through countless summer nights a vanished
      throng,
Only the Indian camp-fire flickered low.
The odor of the baleful cigarette
Assails us now, where the mild calumet
Around the circle like a censer swung.
The notes of Strauss intoxicate the air,
And dainty feet in cadence twinkle there,
Where in rude strains the warriors' deeds were
      sung,
And where the Indian lover's plaintive flute
Lured to the trysting-place the dusky maid.

3

Discreetly hidden in the sylvan shade,
The Anglomaniac comes to press his suit,
And Patrick, too, out for a holiday,
Strolls with his Bridget here *en dimanché*,
And softly whispers in his charmer's ear
The same old tale, to lovers ever dear.
The rustling leaves, the waves, the mating bird,
Sing the same songs the Indian maiden heard.

Save a few stately names, the vanished race
Whose dust we daily trample leave no trace
Or monument.   None who that race have known
Ere poisoned by the vices of our own,
Deem it ignoble ; but the white man's breath,
To him a besom of consuming death,
Sweeps him like ashes from his natal hearth,
E'en as one day some race of stronger birth
Will sweep our children's children from the earth.
More noxious than the fabled upas tree,
We blight his virtues first, and then with scorn
Repel the hands extended once to save
Our exiled fathers, fleeing o'er the wave.
Yet in his deepest fall, the warrior, born
Of warrior lineage fetterless and free,
Retains unquenched in his unyielding soul
A secret flame in spite of all control.
He brooks no slavish, ignominious toil,
By scourger driven to till the white man's soil.
Chained in Plutonian caverns far from day,

His spirit swiftly chafes its bars away ;
Or by his own impatient hand released,
With rapture bounds as to a marriage feast.
Wealth, pomp, and power ne'er his soul affect ;
Still unabashed he stands, unmoved, erect,
His blanket draped, albeit not too clean,
About him with a Roman consul's mien,
And in the white light of a throne his eye
Would meet, nor quail, the eye of majesty.
His own war-eagle to the sun that soared,
Gave back with eye undimmed its fiery glare, ·
And sported with the speaking lightnings where
The Thunder-Birds[1] along the tempest roared ;
Or swept the plain, but saw no Indian slave
From the Pacific to Atlantic wave.

Fair Minnetonka, thou art changed, and yet
I know not if 'twere matter for regret.
Thou wast a maid untried, with yielding heart,
With flowing hair, and ample sheltering arms,
And unabashed contours, whose rosy charms
Were all untrammelled by the hand of art,
And eyes of dreamy mystery, wherein
E'en then thy triumphs dimly were foreseen ;
A worldly-wise and queenly woman now,
Adorned with spoil of many victories,

---

[1] Thunder-Bird, a supernatural winged creature which
causes thunder and lightning by the flapping of its
wings and the winking of its eyes.

And flush of further conquest on thy brow ;
Jewels cannot thy native charms enhance.
Nor can thy robes, too tightly laced perchance,
The matchless beauty of thy form disguise.
Through every change, by every tongue confessed,
Peerless amid thy sisters East or West :
Like her of whom the master-singer wrote,
" Age cannot wither her nor custom stale
Her infinite variety."

           Thus float
My wandering thoughts, as on the balcony
I sit alone bathed in the moonlight pale,
And musing thus the scene changed suddenly :
Hotel and cottage vanished ; to the shore
The prairie sloped a green unbroken floor.
Eight lustrums back, through rosy summers fled,
Adown a dwindling vista far I sped.
A careless youth : again my hoary head
Bloomed with the sunny wealth of twenty years.
A day came back, a day without compeers,
When with a bright companion long since dead,
In my canoe I flitted o'er the lake,
And our swift paddles scattered pearly tears
Upon the smiling ripples in our wake.

She, my companion, was a little maid
Of somewhat rustic garb, of English speech,
Yet something in her accents quaint and rich,
And the warm tinge upon her cheek, betrayed

The mingling crimson of a darker shade,—
Her kinship to the remnant lingering still,
Whose cone-shaped lodges picturesquely stood,
Dotting the hither base of yonder hill,
Like late leaves clinging, spite of growing chill,
Upon the boughs of a November wood.
Changing our mood, we idly drifted there,
Two happy children in a cradling shell
Poised 'twixt two azure vaults : the mystic spell
Of Indian summer brooded in the air,
Filling with human love and sympathy
E'en things inanimate ; the earth and sky
Leaned to each other, and the rocks and trees,
Like brothers, seemed sharing our reveries.

"Tell me some legend of the lake," I cried,
"For in a spot that breathes on every side
Such air of poesy, whose influence
Subdues with such a charm our every sense,
How many loving hearts have loved and died !
How many souls as lofty and intense
As those whose names throughout the whole world
    ring,
In the high songs the olden minstrels sing !
Who hears those voices e'en but for a day,
The sound remains a part of him alway :
Penelope the constant ; Hero sweet ;
Briseis weeping at Achilles' feet ;
Andromeda by wingèd Perseus found—

Bright blossom to the sea-girt rock fast bound ;
The Lesbian queen of song, but passion's slave,
Who quenched her burning torch beneath the
    wave ;
Helen, whose beauty, like a fatal brand,
Lit up the towers of Troy o'er sea and land ;
And Juliet, swaying at her window's height,
What slender lily in the wan moonlight."

" I do not know," the little maid replied,
"The names of which you speak, but ere she
    died
My mother told me many stories old,
Some joyous and some sad, of warriors bold,
And spirits, haunting forest, plain, and stream.
Each had its god, and creatures of strange form,
Half beast, half human ; all these figures seem
Mingling away in a fantastic swarm,
Dim as the faces of a last year's dream,
Or motes that mingle in a slant sunbeam.
The legends vanish too ; among them all
This one alone, distinctly I recall."

The tale she told me then I now rehearse,
Set in a frame of rude, unpolished verse.

PART I.

Winona,[1] first-born daughter, was the name
Of a Dakota girl who, long ago,
Dwelt with her people here unknown to fame.
Sweet word, Winona, how my heart and lips
Cling to that name (my mother's was the same
Ere her form faded into death's eclipse),
Cling lovingly, and loth to let it go.
All arts that unto savage life belong
She knew, made moccasins, and dressed the game.
From crippling fashions free, her well-knit frame
At fifteen summers was mature and strong.
She pitched the tipi,[2] dug the tipsin [3] roots,
Gathered wild rice and store of savage fruits.
Fearless and self-reliant, she could go
Across the prairie on a starless night ;
She speared the fish while in his wildest flight,
And almost like a warrior drew the bow.
Yet she was not all hardness : the keen glance,
Lighting the darkness of her eyes, perchance
Betrayed no softness, but her voice, that rose
O'er the weird circle of the midnight dance,
Through all the gamut ran of human woes,
Passion, and joy.   A woman's love she had

[1] The name given by the Dakotas to the first-born, if a
female.
[2] Tipi, skin tent.
[3] An edible root found on the prairies.

For ornament ; on gala days was clad
In garments of the softest doeskin fine,
With shells about her neck ; moccasins neat
Were drawn, like gloves, upon her little feet,
Adorned with scarlet quills of porcupine.
Innocent of the niceties refined
That to the toilet her pale sisters bind,
Yet much the same beneath the outer rind,
She was, though all unskilled in bookish lore,
A sound, sweet woman to the very core.

Winona's uncle, and step-father too,
Was all the father that she ever knew ;
By the Absarakas[1] her own was slain
Before her memory could his face retain.
Two bitter years his widow mourned him dead,
And then his elder brother she had wed.
None loved Winona's uncle ; he was stern
And harsh in manner, cold and taciturn,
And none might see, without a secret fear,
Those thin lips ever curling to a sneer.
And yet he was of note and influence
Among the chieftains ; true he rarely lent
More than his presence in the council tent,
And when he rose to speak disdained pretence
Of arts rhetoric, but his few words went

[1] The Crow Indians, hereditary foes of the Dakotas,
call themselves Absaraka, which means crow in their
language.

Straight and incisive to the question's core,
And rarely was his counsel overborne.
The Raven was the fitting name he bore,
And though his winters wellnigh reached three-
score,
Few of his tribe excelled him in the chase.
A warrior of renown, but never wore
The dancing eagle plumes, and seemed to scorn
The vanities and follies of his race.

I said the Raven was beloved by none ;
But no, among the elders there was one
Who often sought him, and the two would walk
Apart for hours, and converse alone.
The gossips, marvelling much what this might
mean,
Whispered that they at midnight had been seen
Far from the village wrapped in secret talk.
They seemed in truth an ill-assorted brace,
But Nature oft in Siamese bond unites,
By some strange tie, the farthest opposites.
Gray Cloud was oily, plausible, and vain,
A conjurer with subtle scheming brain ;
Too corpulent and clumsy for the chase,
His lodge was still provided with the best,
And though sometimes but a half welcome guest,
He took his dish and spoon to every feast.[1]

[1] Each Indian guest at a banquet carries with him his
own wooden bowl and horn spoon.

Priestcraft and leechcraft were combined in him,
Two trades occult upon which knaves have
    thriven,
Almost since man from Paradise was driven;
Padding with pompous phrases worn and old
Their scanty esoteric science dim,
And gravely selling, at their weight in gold,
Placebos colored to their patients' whim.
Man's noblest mission here too oft is made,
In heathen as in Christian lands, a trade.
Holy the task to comfort and console
The tortured body and the sin-sick soul,
But pain and sorrow, even prayer and creed,
Are turned too oft to instruments of greed.
The conjurer claimed to bear a mission high :
Mysterious omens of the earth and sky
He knew to read ; his medicine could find
In time of need the buffalo, and bind
In sleep the senses of the enemy.
Perhaps not wholly a deliberate cheat,
And yet dissimulation and deceit
Oozed from his form obese at every pore.
Skilled by long practice in the priestly art,
To chill with superstitious fear the heart,
And versed in all the legendary lore,
He knew each herb and root that healing bore ;
But lest his flock might grow as wise as he,
Disguised their use with solemn mummery.
When all the village wrapped in slumber lay,

His midnight incantations often fell,
His chant now weirdly rose, now sank away,
As o'er some dying child he cast his spell.
And sometimes through his frame strange tremors
    ran—
Magnetic waves, swept from the unknown pole
Linking the body to the wavering soul ;
And swifter came his breath, as if to fan
The feeble life spark, and his finger tips
Were to the brow of pain like angel lips.
No wonder if in moments such as these
He half believed in his own deities,
And thought his sacred rattle could compel
The swarming powers unseen to serve him well.

The Raven lay one evening in his tent
With his accustomed crony at his side ;
Around their heads a graceful aureole
Of.smoke curled upward from the scarlet bowl
Of Gray Cloud's pipe with willow bark supplied.
Winona's thrifty mother came and went,
Her form with household cares and burdens bent,
Fresh fuel adds, and stirs the boiling pot.
Meanwhile the young Winona, half reclined,
Plies her swift needle, that resource refined
For woman's leisure, whatsoe'er her lot,
The kingly palace or the savage cot.

The cronies smoked without a sign or word,
Passing the pipe sedately to and fro ;

Only a distant wail of hopeless woe,
A mother mourning for her child, was heard,
And Gray Cloud moved, as though the sound had
    stirred
Some dusty memory ; still that bitter wail,
Rachel's despairing cry without avail,
That beats the brazen firmament in vain,
Since the first mother wept o'er Abel slain.
At length the conjurer's lips the silence broke,
Softly at first as to himself he spoke,
Till warmed by his own swarming fancies' brood
He poured the strain almost in numbers rude.

THE COMBAT BETWEEN THE THUNDER-BIRDS AND THE WATER-DEMONS.

Gray Cloud shall not be as other men,
Dull clods that move and breathe a day or two,
Ere other clods shall bury them from view.
Tempest and sky have been my home, and when
I pass from earth I shall find welcome there.
Sons of the Thunder-Bird my playmates were,
Ages ago [1] (the tallest oak to-day
In all the land was but a grass blade then).
Reared with such brethren, breathing such an air,
My spirit grew as tall and bold as they ;

[1] Many Indians believe in the transmigration of souls, and some of them profess to remember previous states of existence.

We tossed the ball and flushed the noble prey
O'er happy plains from human footsteps far ;
And when our high chief's voice to arm for war
Rang out in tones that rent the morning sky,
None of the band exulted more than I.

A god might gaze and tremble at the sight
Of our array that turned the day to night;
With bow and shield and flame-tipped arrows all,
Rushing together at our leader's call,
Like storm clouds sweeping round a mountain
    height.
The lofty cliffs our warlike muster saw,
Hard by the village of great Wabashaw,[1]
Where through a lake the Mississippi flows ;
Far o'er the dwelling of our ancient foes,
The hated Water-Demon [2] and his sons,
Cold, dark and deep the sluggish current runs.

Up from their caverns swarming, when they heard
The rolling signal of the Thunder-Bird,
The Water-Demon and his sons arose,
And answered back the challenge of their foes.
With horns tumultuous clashing like a herd
Of warring elks that struggle for the does,
They lashed the wave to clouds of spray and
    foam,

[1] A renowned chief formerly living on Lake Pepin.
[2] A supernatural monster inhabiting the larger rivers
and lakes, and hereditary foe of the Thunder-Bird.

Through which their forms uncouth, like buffa-
    loes
Seen dimly through a morning mist, did loom,
Or isles at twilight rising from the shore.

Though we were thirty, they at least fourscore,
We rushed upon them, and a midnight pall
Over the seething lake our pinions spread,
'Neath which our gleaming arrows thickly sped,
As shooting stars that in the rice-moon fall.
Rent by our beating wings the cloud-waves swung
In eddies round us, and our leader's roar
Smote peal on peal, and from their bases flung
The rocks that towered along the trembling shore.

A Thunder-Bird—alas, my chosen friend,
But even so a warrior's life should end,—
A Thunder-Bird was stricken ; his bright beak,
Cleaving the tumult like a lightning streak,
Smote with a fiery hiss the watery plain ;
His upturned breast, where gleamed one fleck of
    red,
His sable wings, one moment wide outspread,
Blackened the whirlpool o'er his sinking head.

The Water-Demon's sons by scores were slain
By our swift arrows falling like the rain ;
With yells of rage they sank beneath the wave
That ran all redly now, but could not save.

We asked not mercy, mercy never gave;
Our flaming darts lit up the farthest caves,
Fathoms below the reach of deepest line ;
Our cruel spears, taller than mountain pine,
Mingled their life blood with the ruddy wave.

The combat ceased, the Thunder-Birds had won.
The Water-Demon with one favorite son
Fled from the carnage and escaped our wrath.
The vapors, thinly curling from the shore,
Faint musky odors to our nostrils bore.
The air was stilled, the silence of the dead ;
The sun, just starting on his downward path,
A rosy mantle o'er the prairie shed,
Save where, like vultures, ominous and still,
We clustered close, on sullen wings outspread ;
And sometimes, with a momentary chill,
A giant shadow swept o'er plain and hill,—
A Thunder-Bird careering overhead,
Seeking the track by which the foe had fled.

While thus we hovered motionless, the sun
Adown the west his punctual course had run,
When lo, two shining points far up the stream
That split the prairie with a silver seam,—
The fleeing Water-Demon and his son ;
Like icicles they glittered in the beam
Still struggling up from the horizon's rim.
His sleeping anger kindled at the sight,
Our leader's eyes glowed like a flaming brand.

2

Thrilled by one impulse, all our sable band
Dove through the gathering shadows of the
    night
On wings outshaken for a headlong flight.
Anger, revenge, but more than all the thirst,
The glorious emulation to be first,
Stung me like fire, and filled each quivering
    plume.
With tenfold speed our sharp beaks cleft the
    gloom,
A swarm of arrows singing to the mark,
We hissed to pierce the foe ere yet 't was dark.

Still up the stream the Water-Demons fled,
Their bodies glowed like fox-fire far ahead ;
But every moment saw the distance close
Between our thirsting spear-heads and our foes.
Louder the blast our buzzing pinions made
Than mighty forest in a whirlwind swayed ;
The giant cliffs of Redwing speeding back,
Like spectres melting from a cloudy wrack,
Melted from view in our dissolving track.
Kaposia's village, clustered on the shore,
With sound of snapping poles and tipis riven,
Vanished like swan's-down by a tempest driven.
Stung by our flight, the keen air smote us sore
As ragged hailstones ; on, still on, we strained,
And fast and faster on the chase we gained,
But neck and neck the fierce pursuit remained,

Till close ahead we saw the rocky walls
O'er which the mighty river plunging falls,[1]
And at their base the Water-Demons lay :
The panting chase at last had turned to bay.

Then thrilled my nerves with more than mortal
   strength ;
A breath of Deity was in the burst
That bore me out a goodly lance's length
To meet the Water-Demon's son accurst.
His evil horn clanged hollow on my shield
Just as my spear transfixed him through and
   through ;
A moment towering o'er the foam he reeled,
Then sank beneath the roaring falls from view.
A dying yell that haunts me yet he gave,
And as he fell the crippled water coiled
About him like a wounded snake, and boiled,
Lashing itself to madness o'er his grave.

We knew not where the parent Demon fled ;
None of our spears might pierce his ancient mail,
Welded with skill demoniac scale on scale.
Some watery realm he wanders, and 't is said
That he is changed and bears a brighter form,
And goodly sons again about him swarm ;
And peace, 't is but a hollow truce I know,
Now reigns between him and his ancient foe.

[1] The falls of St. Anthony.

He hates me still, and fain would do me harm,
But neither man nor demon dares offend,
Who hath the cruel Thunder-Bird for friend.

PART II.

Nature hath her *élite* in every land,
Sealed by her signet, felt although unseen.
Winona 'mid her fellows moved a queen,
And scarce a youthful beau in all the band
But sighed in secret longing for her hand.
One only she distinguished o'er the rest,
The latest aspirant for martial fame,
Redstar, a youth whose coup-stick like his name
(Till recently he had been plain Chaské) [1]
Was new, fresh plucked the feathers on his crest.
Just what the feats on which he based his claim
To warlike glory it were hard to say ;
He ne'er had seen more than one trivial fray,
But bold assurance sometimes wins the day.
Winona gave him generous credit, too,
For all the gallant deeds he meant to do.
His gay, barbaric dress, his lofty air
Enmeshed her in a sweet bewildering snare.
Transfigured by the light of her own passion,
She saw Chaské in much the usual fashion

[1] The name given to the first-born, if a male. Upon
becoming a warrior or performing some notable feat, the
youth is permitted to select another name.

Of fairer maids, who love, or think they do.
'T is not the man they love, but what he seems;
A bright Hyperion, moving stately through
The rosy ether of exalted dreams.

Alas ! that love, the purest and most real,
Clusters forever round some form ideal ;
And martial things have some strange necro-
    mancy
To captivate romantic maiden fancy.
The very word " Lieutenant " hath a charm,
E'en coupled with a vulgar face and form,
A shrivelled heart and microscopic wit,
Scarce for a coachman or a barber fit ;
His untried sword, his title, are to her
Better than genius, wealth, or high renown ;
His uniform is sweeter than the gown
Of an Episcopalian minister ;
And " dash," for swagger but a synonym,
Is knightly grace and chivalry with him.

Unnoted young Winona's passion grew,
Chaské alone the tender secret knew ;
And he, too selfish love like hers to know,
Warmed by her presence to a transient glow,
Her silent homage drank as 't were his due.
Winona asked no more though madly fond,
Nor hardly dreamed as yet of closer bond ;

But Chance, or Providence, or iron Fate
(Call it what name you will), or soon or late,
Bends to its purpose every human will,
And brings to each its destined good or ill.

THE GROVE.

O'erlooking Minnetonka's shore,
A grove enchanted lured of yore,
Lured to their deepest woe and joy,
A happy maiden and careless boy ;
Lured their feet to its inmost core,
Where like snowy maidens the aspen trees
Swayed and beckoned in the breeze,
While the prairie grass, like rippling seas,
Faintly murmuring lulling hymns,
Rippled about their gleaming limbs.

There is no such charm in a garden-close,
However fair its bower and rose,
As a place where the wild and free rejoice.
Nor doth the storied and ivied arch
Woo the heart with half so sweet a voice
As the bowering arms of the wild-wood larch,
Where the clematis and wild woodbine
Festoon the flowering eglantine ;
Where in every flower, shrub, and tree
Is heard the hum of the honey-bee,
And the linden blossoms are softly stirred,
As the fanning wings of the humming-bird

Scatter a perfume of pollen dust,
That mounts to the kindling soul like must ;
Where the turtles each spring their loves renew—
The old, old story, " coo-roo, coo-roo,"
Mingles with the wooing note
That bubbles from the song-bird's throat ;
Where on waves of rosy light at play,
Mingle a thousand airy minions,
And drifting as on a golden bay,
The butterfly with his petal pinions,
From isle to isle of his fair dominions
Floats with the languid tides away ;
Where the squirrel and rabbit shyly mate,
And none so timid but finds her fate ;
The meek hen-robin upon the nest
Thrills to her lover's flaming breast.
Youth, Love, and Life, 'mid scenes like this,
Go to the same sweet tune of bliss ;
E'en the flaming flowers of passion seem
Pure as the lily buds that dream
On the bosom of a mountain stream.

Such was the grove that lured of yore,
O'erlooking Minnetonka's shore,
Lured to their deepest woe and joy
A happy maiden and careless boy,—
Lured their feet to its inmost core ;
Where still mysterious shadows slept,
While the plenilune from her path above

With liquid amber bathed the grove,
That through the tree-tops trickling crept,
And every tender alley swept.
The happy maiden and careless boy,
Caught for a moment their deepest joy,
And the iris hues of Youth and Love,
A tender glamour about them wove ;
But the trembling shadows the aspens cast
From the maiden's spirit never passed ;
And the nectar was poisoned that thrilled and
    filled,
From every treacherous leaf distilled,
Her veins that night with a strange alloy.

Swift came the hour that maid and boy must part ;
A glow unwonted, tinged with dusky red
Winona's conscious face as home she sped ;
And to the song exultant in her heart,
Beat her light moccasins with rhythmic tread.
But at the summit of a little hill,
Along whose base the village lay outspread,
A sudden sense of some impending ill
Smote the sweet fever in her veins with chill.
The lake she skirted, on whose mailèd breast
Rode like a shield the moon from out the west.
She neared her lodge, but there her quick eye
    caught
The voice of Gray Cloud, and her steps were
    stayed,

For over her of late an icy fear
Brooded with vulture wings when he was near.

She knew not why, her eye he never sought,
Nor deigned to speak, and yet she felt dismayed
At thought of him, as the mimosa's leaf
Before the fingers touch it shrinks with dread.
She paused a moment, then with furtive tread
Close to the tipi glided like a thief ;
With lips apart, and eager bended head,
She listened there to what the conjurer said.

His voice, low, musical, recounted o'er
Strange tales of days when other forms he wore :
How, far above the highest airy plain
Where soars and sings the weird, fantastic crane,
Wafted like thistle-down he strayed at will,
With power almost supreme for good or ill,
Over all lands and nations near and far,
Beyond the seas, or 'neath the northern star,
And long had pondered where were best to dwell
When he should deign a human shape to wear.
" Whether to be of them that buy and sell,
With fish-scale eyes, and yellow corn-silk hair,
Or with the stone-men chase the giant game.
But wander where you may, no land can claim
A sky so fair as ours ; the sun each day
Circles the earth with glaring eye, but sees
No lakes or plains so beautiful as these ;

Nor e'er hath trod or shall upon the earth
A race like ours of true Dakota birth.
Our chiefs and sages, who so wise as they
To counsel or to lead in peace or war,
And heal the sick by deep mysterious law.
Our beauteous warriors lithe of limb and strong,
Fierce to avenge their own and others' wrong,
What gasping terror smites their battle song
When, night-birds gathering near the dawn of
    day,
Or wolves in chorus ravening for the prey,
They burst upon the sleeping Chippeway ;[1]
Their women wail whose hated fingers dare
To reap the harvest of our midnight hair ;
Swifter than eagles, as a panther fleet,
A hungry panther seeking for his meat,
So swift and noiseless their avenging feet.

    .   .   .   .   .   .

Dakota matrons truest are and best,
Dakota maidens too are loveliest.''

He ceased, and soon, departing through the
    night,
She watched his burly form till out of sight.
And then the Raven spoke in whispers low :
'' Gray Cloud demands our daughter's hand, and
    she

        [1] Hereditary foe of the Dakotas.

Unto his tipi very soon must go.''
Winona's mother sought to make reply,
But something checked her in his tone or eye.
Again the Raven spoke, imperiously :
'' Winona is of proper age to wed ;
Her suitor suits me, let no more be said.''

Winona heard no more ; a rising wave
Of mingled indignation, fear, and shame
Like a resistless tempest shook her frame,
The earth swam round her, and her senses reeled ;
Better for her a thousand times the grave
Than life in Gray Cloud's tent, but what could
  she
Against the stern, implacable decree
Of one whose will was never known to yield ?

Winona fled, scarce knowing where or how ;
Fled like a phantom through the moonlight cool
Until she stood upon the rocky brow
That overlooked a deep sequestered pool,
Where slumbering in a grove-encircled bay
Lake Minnetonka's purest waters lay.
Unto the brink she rushed, but faltered there—
Life to the young is sweet ; in vain her eye
Swept for a moment grove and wave and sky
With mute appeal. But see, two white swans fair
Gleamed from the shadows that o'erhung the
  shore,

Like moons emerging from a sable screen;
Swimming abreast, what haughty king and queen,
With arching necks their regal course they bore.
Winona marvelled at the unwonted sight
Of white swans swimming there at dead of night,
Her frenzy half beguiling with the scene.
Unearthly heralds sure, for in their wake
What ruddy furrows seamed the placid lake.
Almost beneath her feet they came, so near
She might have tossed a pebble on their backs,
When lo, their long necks pierced the waters
    clear,
As down they dove, two shafts of purest light,
And chasing fast on their descending tracks,
A swarm of spirals luminous and white,
Swirled to the gloom of nether depths from sight.

Then all was still for some few moments' space,
So smooth the pool, so vanished every trace,
It seemed that surely the fantastic pair
Had been but snowy phantoms passing there.
Winona hardly hoped to see them rise,
But while she gazed with half expectant eyes,
The waters strangely quivered in a place
About the bigness of a tipi's space,
Where weirdly lighting up the hollow wave
Beat a deep-glowing heart, whose pulsing ray
Now faded to a rosy flush away,
Now filled with fiery glare the farthest cave.

A shapeless bulk arose, then, taking form,
Bloomed forth upon the bosom of the lake
A crystal rose, or hillock mammiform,
And round its base the curling foam did break
As round a sunny islet in a storm ;
And on it poised a swiftly changing form,
With filmy mantle falling musical,
And colors of the floating bubble's ball,
Fair and elusive as the sprites that play,
Bright children of the sun-illumined spray,
'Mid rainbows of a mountain waterfall.
Then mingling with the falling waters came
In whispers sibilant Winona's name ;
So indistinct and low that voice intense,
That she, half frightened, cowering in the grass
In much bewilderment at what did pass,
Till thrice repeated noted not its sense.

She rose, and on the very brink defined,
Against the sky in silhouette outlined,
Erect before the Water-Demon stood.
Again those accents weird her wonder stirred,
And this is what the listening maiden heard :
" Thy fate, Winona, hangs on thine own choice
To scorn or heed the Water-Demon's voice.
Gone are thy pleasant days of maidenhood,
And evil hours draw nigh, but knowest thou not,
That what thou fleest is the common lot
Of all thy sisters ? Thou must be the bride

Of one thou lovest not, must toil for him,
Watch for his coming, and endure his whim ;
Must share his tent, and lying at his side
Weep for another till thine eyes grow dim.
And he, so fondly loved, will pass thee by
Indifferent with cold averted eye ;
E'en he, whose wanton hands and hated arms
Have crushed the fair flower of thy maidenhood,
Will weary of thy swiftly fading charms,
And seek another when thy beauty wanes.
Aha, thou shudderest ; in thy tense veins,
Fierce and rebellious, leaps the mingling blood
Of countless warriors, high of soul and brave ;
And would'st thou quench their spirit 'neath the
　　　wave ?
Is Gray Cloud's life more dear to thee than
　　　thine ?
The village sleeps, unguarded is his tent,
Thy knife is keen, and unto thee is lent
A spell to-night of potency malign.
Cradled in blissful dreams alone he lies,
And he shall stray so deep in sleep's dominions,
He would not waken though the rushing pinions
Of his own Thunder-Bird should shake the sky.
All freedom-loving spirits are with thee,
Strike hard and fear not as thou would'st be free ;
Lest thine own hatred prove too weak a charm,
The　Water-Demon's　hate　shall　nerve　thine
　　　arm.''

The Water-Demon sank and disappeared,
And faint and fainter fell those accents weird,
Until the air was silent as the grave,
Still as December's crystal seal the wave.
Homeward again Winona took her way.
How changed in one short hour ! no longer now
The song-birds singing at her heart, but there
A thousand gnashing furies made their lair,
And urged her on ; her nearest pathway lay
Over a little hill, and on its brow
A group of trees, whereof each blackened bough
Bore up to heaven as if in protest mute
Its clustering load of ghostly charnel fruit,[1]
The swaddled forms of all the village dead—
Maid, lusty warrior, and toothless hag,
The infant and the conjurer with his bag,
Peacefully rotting in their airy bed.
As on a battle plain she saw them lie,
Fouling the fairness of the moonlit sky ;
And heavily there flapped above her head,
Some floating drapery or tress of hair,
Loading with pestilential breath the air
That fanned her temples, or the reeking wing
Of unclean bird obscenely hovering ;
And something crossed her path that halting
    nigh,

[1] The Dakotas formerly disposed of their dead by fasten-
ing them to the branches of trees, or to rude platforms.
This is still practised to some extent.

At the intruder glared with evil eye,—
She hardly heeded passing swiftly by.

Leaving behind that hideous umbrage fast,
What wraith escaping from its tenement,
Winona through the sleeping village passed,
And pausing not, to Gray Cloud's tipi went,
Laid back the door, and with a stealthy tread,
Entered and softly crouched beside his head.
Her gaze that seemed to pierce his inmost thought,
Keen as the ready knife her hand had sought,
And through the open door the slant moonbeams
Smiting the sleeper's face awaked him not.
He vaguely muttered in his wandering dreams
Of " medicine," and of the Thunder-Bird.
As if to go, her knife she half returned ;
Whether her woman's heart with pity stirred,
Or superstitious awe, she slightly turned,
But gazing still, over his features came
The semblance of a smile, and his arms moved,
Clasping in rosy dreams some form beloved,
And his lips moved, and though no sound she
      heard,
She thought they shaped her name, and a red
      flame
Leaped to her brain, and through her vision
      passed ;
A raging demon seized and filled her frame,
And like a lightning flash leaped forth her knife :

That cold keen heart-pang is his last of life ;
The Water-Demon is avenged at last.

PART III.

She struck but once, no need hath lightning stroke
For second blow to rend the heart of oak,
Nor waited there to see how Gray Cloud died ;
Her fury all in that fierce outburst spent,
As from a charnel cave she fled the tent ;
The wolfish dog suspiciously outside
Sniffed at her moccasins but let her pass.
Her tipi soon she reached, distant no more
Than arrow from a warrior's bowstring sent,
Paused but to wipe her knife upon the grass,
And found her usual couch upon the floor.
But not to sleep ; she closed her eyes in vain,
Shutting away the moonlight from her view ;
Darkness and moonlight wore the same dread
      hue,
Flooding the universe with crimson stain.
She clasped her bosom with her hands to still
The throbbing of her heart that seemed to fill
With tell-tale echoes all the air ; an owl
The secret with unearthly shrieks confessed,
And Gray Cloud's dog sent forth a doleful howl
At intervals ; but worse than all the rest,
That dreadful drum still beating in her breast,
As furious war-drums in the scalp-dance beat
To the mad circling of delirious feet.

3

Early next morning, as the first faint rays
Of sunlight through the rustling lindens played,
Two children sent to seek the conjurer's aid,
Gazed on the sight, with horror and amaze,
Of Gray Cloud's lifeless body rolled in blood.
Fast through the village spread the news, and
    stirred
With mingled fear and wonder all who heard.
The oracles were baffled and dismayed,
And spoke with muffled tones and looks of dread :
" Some envious foeman lurking in the wood,
With medicine more strong than his," they said,
" Stole in last night and gave the fatal wound."
The warriors scoured the country miles around,
Seeking for sign or trail, but naught they found :
The murderer left behind no clue or trace
More than a vampire's flight through darkling
    space.

The Raven with a stoic calmness heard
Of Gray Cloud's death, nor showed by look or
    word
The wrath that to its depth his being stirred.
Winona heard the news with false surprise,
As if just roused from sleep she rubbed her eyes ;
When she arose her knees like aspens shook,
But this she quelled and forced a tranquil look
To feign the calmness that her soul forsook.
And when the mourning wail rose on the air,
Winona's voice was heard commingling there.

She gathered with the other maidens where,
On a rude bier, the conjurer's body lay
Adorned and decked in funeral array.
She flung a handful of her sable hair,
And wept such tears above the painted clay [1]
As weeps a youthful widow, only heir,
Over the coffin of a millionaire.

Moons waxed to fulness and to sickles waned.
The gossips still conversed with bated breath.
The appalling mystery of Gray Cloud's death,
Wrapped in impenetrable gloom, remained
A blighting shadow o'er the village spread.
But youthful spirits are invincible,
Nor fear nor superstition long can quell
The bubbling flow of that perennial well ;
And so the youths and maidens soon regained
The wonted gayety that late had fled.
All save Winona, in whose face and mien,
Unto the careless eye, no change was seen ;
But one that noted might sometimes espy
A furtive fear that shot across her eye,
As in a forest, 'thwart some bit of blue,
Darts a rare bird that shuns the hunter's view.
Her laugh, though gay, a subtle change con-
    fessed,
And in her attitude a vague unrest

---

[1] The Indians paint and adorn a body before sepulture.

Betrayed a world of feelings unexprest.
A shade less light her footsteps in the dance,
And sometimes now the Raven's curious glance
Her soul with terrors new and strange oppressed.

Grief shared is lighter, none had she to share
Burdens that grew almost too great to bear,
For Redstar sometimes seemed to look askance,
And sought, they said, to win another breast.
Winona feigned to laugh, but in her heart
The rumor rankled like a poisoned dart.
Sometimes she almost thought the Raven guessed
The guilty secrets that her thoughts oppressed,
And sought, whene'er she could, to shun his sight.
Apart from human kind, still more and more,
The Raven dwelt, and human speech forbore.
And once upon a wild tempestuous night,
When all the demons of the earth and air
Like raging furies were embattled there,
She, peering fearfully, amid the swarm
Flitting athwart the flashes of the storm,
By fitful gleams beheld the Raven's form.
To her he spoke not since the fateful night
His chosen comrade passed from human sight,
Save only once, forgetting he was by
And half forgetting too her cares and woes,
Unto her lips some idle jest arose.
"Winona," said the Raven, in a tone
Of stern reproof that on the instant froze

All thought of mirth, and when she met his eye,
As by a serpent's charm it fixed her own ;
The hate and anger of a soul intense
Were all compressed in that remorseless glance,
The coldly cruel meaning of whose sense
Smote down the shield of her false innocence.
She strove to wrest her eye from his in vain,
Held by that gaze ophidian like a bird,
As in a trance she neither breathed nor stirred.
And gazing thus an icy little lance,
Smaller than quill from wing of humming-bird,
Shot from his eyes, and a keen stinging pain
Sped through the open windows of her brain.
Her senses failed, she sank upon the ground,
And darkness veiled her eyes ; she never knew
How long this was, but when she slowly grew
Back from death's counterfeit, and looked around,
So little change was there, that it might seem
The scene had been but a disordered dream.
The Raven sat in his accustomed place,
Smoking his solitary pipe ; his face,
A gloomy mask that none might penetrate,
Betrayed no sign of anger, grief, or hate ;
Absorbed so deep in thoughts that none might
    share,
He noted not Winona's presence there ;
From his disdainful lips the thin blue smoke
From time to time in little spirals broke,
Floating like languid sneers upon the air,

And settling round him in a veil of blue
So sinister to her disordered view,
That she arose and quickly stole away.
She shunned him more than ever from that day,
And never more unmoved could she behold
That countenance inscrutable and cold.

But Hope and Love, like Indian summer's glow,
Gilding the prairies ere December's snow,
Lit with a transient beam Winona's eye.
The season for the Maidens' Dance drew nigh,
And Redstar vowed, whatever might betide,
To claim her on the morrow as his bride.
What now to her was all the world beside ?
The evil omens darkening all her sky,
Malicious sneers, her rival's envious eye,
While her false lover lingered at her side,
All passed like thistle-down unheeded by.

The evening for the dance arrived at last ;
An ancient crier through the village passed,
And summoned all the maidens to repair
To the appointed place, a greensward where,
Since last year unprofaned by human feet,
Rustled the prairie grass and flowers sweet.
None but the true and pure might enter there—
Maidens whose souls unspotted had been kept.
At set of sun the circle there was formed,
And thitherward the happy maidens swarmed.

The people gathered round to view the scene :
Old men in broidered robes that trailing swept,
And youths in all their finery arrayed,
Dotting like tropic birds the prairie green,
Their rival graces to the throng displayed.
Winona came the last, but as she stept
Into the mystic ring one word, " Beware ! "
Rang out in such a tone of high command
That all was still, and every look was turned
To where the Raven stood ; his stern eye burned,
And like a flower beneath that withering glare
She faded fast. No need that heavy hand
To lead Winona from the joyous band ;
No need those shameful words that stained the air :
" Let not the sacred circle be defiled
By one who, all too easily beguiled,
Beneath her bosom bears a warrior's child."

Winona swiftly fleeing, as she passed,
One look upon her shrinking lover cast
That scared his coward heart for many a day,
Into the deepest woods she took her way.
The dance was soon resumed, and as she fled,
Like hollow laughter chasing overhead,
Pursued the music and the maidens' song.
Just as she passed from sight an angry eye
Glared for a moment from the western sky,
And flung one quivering shaft of dazzling white,
With tenfold thunder-peal, adown the night.

Her mother followed her, and sought her long,
Calling and listening through the falling dew,
While fast and furious still the cadence grew
Of the gay dance, whose distant music fell,
Smiting the mother like a funeral knell.
High rode the sun in heaven next day before
The stricken mother found along the shore
The object of her unremitting quest.
The cooling wave whereon she lay at rest
Had stilled the tumult of Winona's breast.
Along that shapely ruin's plastic grace,
And in the parting of her braided hair,
The hopeless mother's glances searching there
The Thunder-Bird's mysterious mark might trace.

So died Winona, and let all beware,
For vengeance follows fast and will not spare,
Nor maid, nor warrior that dares offend
Who hath the cruel Thunder-Bird for friend.

MISCELLANEOUS POEMS

TO A YOUNG MAN.

CARESS thy pleasures with a reverent touch,
   Too soon at best their early fragrance flees.
Seek not to know, to see, or taste too much :
   The sweetest, deepest cup hath still its lees ;
The blushing grape is not too rudely pressed,
When gushes forth its richest and its best.

Bird, bubble, butterfly on light wing straying,
   With changing tints of crimson, blue, and gold,
Upon warm waves of summer sunlight swaying,
   When thy frail, flaming wing the boy shall hold,
Alas, how soon its fragile charms expire !
E'en so when strong men seize their soul's desire.

Rend not with ruthless hand the lily's bell,
   To gather all its sweetness at a breath ;
Spill not the pearl deep in its bosom's cell,
   The crystal gift Aurora's tears bequeath.
So shall a delicate perfume be thine,
Through all the weary hours of day's decline.

The gentlest spirits of the earth and air—
　Sweet mysteries to ruder men unknown—
Will yield delights as delicate as rare,
　The secret bowers of Love shall be thy own,
The one great bliss, so long thy hope's despair,
Will press with eager feet to find thee there.

TELL ME, DEAR BIRD.

IN the warm twilight where I mused, there
came
A bird of unknown race with breast of flame.

Tell me, dear bird, O bird with breast of flame,
I conjure thee, e'en by his sacred name,
How may I lure and win Love to my side?
There is no lure for Love, in patience bide,
And if he cometh not await him still,
Love cometh only when and where he will.

But when he cometh, bird with breast of flame,
Teach me his roving feet to bind and tame.
Many have sought to bind him, but in vain;
He will not brook nor gold nor silken chain.
If he is caught, Love languishes and dies,
And 't is not Love, if free to stay, he flies.

Tell me, dear bird, O bird with breast of flame,
When true Love comes, how may I know his
name?
What are the golden words upon his tongue:
What message sweeter than a seraph's song?

Love hath no shibboleth, and where are words
For the enraptured songs of summer birds?

Tell me, dear Love, O bird with breast of flame,
The deepest sense and meaning of thy name?
Two all-sufficing souls for woe or bliss,
But what they do, or what their converse is,
Love only knows; they walk where none may see,
Wrapped in the shades of a sweet mystery.

F AR away under Hesper,
  In seas never crossed,
Like a faint-uttered whisper,
  Forgotten and lost ;
Where no sail ever flies
  O'er the face of the deep,
A lost island lies
  Forgotten, asleep.
An island reposes,
  Distant and dim,
Where a cloud-veil of roses
Never uncloses,
Dreams and reposes
  On the horizon's rim.
An island arrayed
  In such magical grace,
It would seem to be made
  For some happier race.
Each valley and bower
  Has a charm of its own ;
A perfume each flower,
  Elsewhere unknown ;

A charm of such power
　That once known to the heart,
If but for an hour,
　It can never depart.
E'en the surges of ocean,
　Ceasing their roar,
Their rage and commotion,
　Sigh in on the shore
With a melody saintly,
　As vespers that seem
Chanted so quaintly,
By sisters so saintly,
Mingling so faintly
　With the voice of a dream.

One summer time olden,
　That standeth alone
With its memories golden,
　That isle was my own.
O island enchanted !
　Where now does she rove—
The bright nymph that haunted
　Thy fountain and grove,
While still at her side,
　Whereever she strayed,
By the mountain or tide,
　My footsteps were stayed ?
Do her pulses still beat
　To the pulses of yore ?

Say, now, do her feet
   Tread some pitiless shore,
Still hoping to meet
   One who cometh no more?

O that summer ! its ray
   In my heart lingers yet,
Long after the day-
   Star it came from has set.
My star of the night
   And of morning was she,
My song-bird, my white-
   Wingèd bark on the sea ;
My rainbow, illuming
   With beauty and light ;
My rose-garden, blooming,
Sweetly perfuming
The hours of the night.

But at last, in its fleetness,
   It seemed that each day
From the charm and the sweetness
   Took something away,
Till the flowers all faded
   From summer's bright crown,
The skies were o'ershadowed,
   The forests were brown.
In the voices of morning
   There crept a new tone,

4

A faint whispered warning
　　From regions unknown,
And over each heart
　　Stole a mystical fear
That our joy would depart
　　With the flight of the year.
A pale, cold, new-comer
　　Had entered our isle,
From a land beyond summer
　　And sunshine and smile,
Subduing us quite,
　　Though we saw not his face,
As winter gives blight
　　When it cometh apace.
Her glances and mine
　　Sought each other no more,
Each fearing some sign
　　Not seen there before.
Yet no word was revealing
　　Misgiving or chill ;
Each sought for concealing
The deathly, congealing
　　Foreboding of ill.

But at last came a night
　　When our last song was sung,
And like children in fright
　　Together we clung.
No farewell was spoken,

Our voices were dumb,
But we knew without token
That parting was come.
In the darkness that bound us
A night-bird did sing,
And the black air around us
Was moved by his wing,
As in vulture waves sweeping
He sped from the shore,
And away from my keeping
My Day-star he tore.

BITTER bewailing
　　Sweet Life's sad failing
Is unavailing
　　Your prayers or mine.
Years onward sweeping
Bring blight for reaping,
For laughter weeping,
　　Wormwood for wine.

The old sweet vision
Comes to derision
The dream Elysian
　　That once was ours.
The rushing river
Mocks our endeavor,
And soon will sever
　　My bark from yours.

One joy shall bide me
Whate'er betide me,
This still shall guide me
　　Till life shall fleet ;
Though friends forsake me,
Fate rudely shake me,

And Time shall break me
Beneath his feet,

No power above me
From this can move me—
My Queen did love me !
 One golden day
Her proud heart found me,
Her arms were around me,
Her red lips crowned me
 A King for aye.

O rapturous meeting !
Thy passionate greeting
Was the high beating
 Of a young soul,
For one full yearning,
Hour spurning,
The fetters burning
 Of Fate's control.

The chilling power
Of rank and dower
That sacred hour
 Soon overcast,
And from our faces
Swept the faint traces
Of those embraces,
 The first and last.

She may recover,
When days are over,
Some happier lover,
    Forsaking me.
I, e'en though hated,
Am consecrated ;
More meanly mated
    Can never be.

Let new flames redden
Where light loves deaden,
Let pulses leaden
    Leap forth anew ;
But on this altar
Till breath shall falter,
Though all else alter,
    Nought shall renew.

LOVE'S TRIBUTES.

O THAT I might inspire my song with power
To crown thy brows with more than queenly
dower ;
To pour on thee a more than golden shower,
And fill thy soul with sunshine every hour.

Time breaks at last the lyre's sweetest strings,
And palls the sweetest note the minstrel sings,
And riches fly away on falcon wings :
Love only to his trust unchanging clings.

Then be my song of whatsoe'er degree,
And gifts however bright and fair to see,
Rare trophies peril won by land and sea,
Yet Love his own chief offering must be.

All that the flower of Love may yield is thine,
From blushing bud to clusters on the vine,
With colors rich as rubies from the mine,
And odors mounting to the soul like wine.

55

But all, I know, is paltry in thine eyes,
So far above them all thy worth doth rise.
In vain my muse with feeble pinions tries
To reach the regions where thy merit lies.

Still o'er Love's treasures hold thy sovereign
    sway ;
Taste them or spill them, keep or cast away ;
By night or daytime, hasten or delay,
Trample them, cull them, go thine own sweet
    way.

THE LITTLE SHEPHERDESS.

PASTORELLE.

L ITTLE lamb, I pray O come to me,
    None to caress and love have I but thee.
Why art thou not some tender shepherd swain,
Then loving thee would ease my weary pain.
My sister Susan, she is fair and tall,
And she may choose among the shepherds all,
And she is called sweet names—my dear, my pet ;
Ah me ! I 'm brown, and I 'm too little yet.

Then stepping forth from a concealing shade,
A youth beyond compare approached the maid,
And, whisp'ring softly in her startled ear,
She heard the tender words, " My pet, my dear."
She blushing stood, confused with downcast eyes,
But heart and face were filled with glad surprise ;
And happier far than Susan tall and fair,
The little nut-brown maiden trembling there.

A FAREWELL.

'T IS true that once I sighed for
    That tender heart of thine ;
I thought I could have died for
    The bliss I now decline.
Too many swains enchanted,
    Since then within that heart,
Have had sweet shelter granted
    For me to claim a part.

Farewell, dear one, thy sorrow,
    Thy tears are all in vain ;
That tender heart to-morrow
    Will find some newer swain.
Thou hast no necromancy
    To restore the passing sway,
Of what was but the fancy
    Of an idle summer day.

TO A FICKLE FAIR ONE.

SOME birds mate three times in a year,
 And I have called thee oft my bird.
I knew not even shame and fear
 Could bind thee long ; take my last word,
 Good-bye, sweet bird.

TO THE SAME.

CONSTANCY and the Phœnix, birds that dwell
 In the bright realms of song, happy his fate
Who elsewhere meets with one, for, mark it well,
Sooner or later he will find its mate.

THE PALACE OF REPOSE.

HELPLESS we start before the break of day,
    And grope along an unknown path our way,
Or follow leaders blind, and many fall ;
But on we press, heedless and joyous all,
As happy fledglings fluttering in the brake,
That nothing reck of prowling fox or snake.
When over us at last the daylight dawns,
We bear the marks of many cruel thorns ;
But brightly on the far horizon gleams
(Of more than earthly grace the vision seems)
The Palace of Repose, that rears on high
Its golden domes against the western sky,
While warm and tender as a poet's dreams,
The restful radiance from each tower that streams.

Now through the early morning air we fly,
As the young shepherd sped with beaming eye
Fast fixed upon the rose-born butterfly.
Toward flowery vales and hills our pathway leads,
But when we reach them all their beauty fades.
Hills that were fairer, ere their paths were won,
Than the long slopes of fountained Helicon,
Are marred by poisonous weeds and flinty stone ;

And forms that seemed, against the distant skies,
Winging their snowy way to Paradise,
Are birds unclean, whose wings are like a breath
From some great charnel-house in lands of death.
And shifting sands beneath our feet are spread,
And pitfalls numberless beset our way,
Where noisome reptiles fill us with dismay ;
On either side lie, fathomless and dim,
Wide plains where wander phantoms stark and
  grim.

Noon comes ; the goal no nearer, on we haste,
Nor note the lengthening shadows of the past.
Luring us on we hear the far, faint moan
Of music, weird and sweet as Memnon's tone,
Heard in the desert by the traveller lone ;
Bewildering as the sounds the shepherds erst
Heard in the vales of Thessaly, when first
Apollo's wondrous music on them burst.
Of all that started with us, hand in hand,
Only a few are left, a dwindling band.
With haggard faces fixed upon the goal,
E'en as the needle to the steadfast pole,
Swifter and swifter, till the evening air
Sings like a serpent through our back-blown hair.
But lo, the night has come,
                    The sun goes down,
His trailing robes with crimson glories crown
The palace we had almost deemed was ours.

Dearer than ever seem those fading towers,
Whose oriel windows gleam like soul-lit eyes
For one bright moment ere thick darkness lies
On earth and sky, then trembling, faint, and sore,
Closing our pathway, lo, we find a door,
The entrance to a narrow house that still
Blocks up the way of every human will.
Wander where'er we may, this self-same goal
Is reached at last by every weary soul.
Our burdens fall unheeded, and our gains,—
This is the end of all our toil and pains.

Over the threshold hangs a shrunken lute,
Upon a tree where grows nor flower nor fruit ;
Bewildering odors fill the heavy air,
The nightshade and the wolf's-bane mingle there ;
The faint perfume of rose and lily, too,
Is swallowed up by asphodel and rue.
We enter in, behold, a lowly bed,
How sweet the poppied perfume o'er it shed,
Where the red poppy swings its censer head.

There sleep shall seize and bind us, sleep su-
        preme,
That knows no waking morn, no troubled dream.
The years shall swiftly cover us from sight,
In silence and insuperable night.

MOODS.

MY wayward youth had drained the cup of
    Life,
Wasting its treasures in the fitful strife,
The mad revolt of a rebellious soul,
That beats the stubborn bars of Fate's control.
My foolish heart whispered, there is no God,
And if there is, let cravens fear his rod :
Be thy own god, slake thy imperious thirst
Where'er thou wilt, no fountain is accurst.
Many strange paths my restless feet had sought,
Not all ignoble, but to each I brought
The turbulence of will that grasps at all,
And, failing, breaks itself against the wall.
Too late I knew my impotence at last,
When the bright glow of youth was overpast.

Worn out, exhausted by the weary route
That leads from knowledge to disgust and doubt,
Defeat, deceit, and baffled purpose stole
Like a corroding canker to my soul.
I hated Life, scorned and despised my kind,
So far astray may err the unbridled mind.

63

I had been nigh to death ; the sullen wave
Already my consenting feet did lave,
When one who thought to be my friend, and fain
Had done me kindness, plucked me back again.
They said my reason wandered, and had found
A peaceful nook remote from sight or sound
Of busy men ; there by the moonlit sea
On a soft couch I lay, where over me
Through the low lattice the sea odors crept,
And from the landward side about me swept
Soft languid waves of amorous perfume,
Of pollen-dust, of bursting bud and bloom.

Wrecked by the storm of life, and cast aside
Like drift rejected by the loathing tide,
Vacant of heart and thought I lay ; the air
That wooed my cheek and gently stirred my hair,
Laden with yearning voices of the spring,
Awoke in me no answering tone or string.

From the deep shadows of the sleeping wood
A baleful night-bird swept the solitude ;
The shuddering moonlight like a living thing
Shrank from the touch of his defiling wing ;
And fiercely following like an eager pack
Of wingèd hounds upon his lurid track,
Lewd mocking spirits filled the thickening air,
Swarming as to a charnel banquet there.
Close at my ear burst forth a piercing yell,

As if each ghoul and fiend from nether hell
Had burst its bonds, and joined that chorus fell ;
My quivering veins and nerves to frenzy stung,
In discord jangled like a harp unstrung.
Suddenly at my heart a quick sharp pluck,
As 't were some foot of small fierce bird had struck
And griped me sore ; then after some short space
The keen pain seized me in another place ;
I felt myself clasped in a rude embrace,
And o'er my body spread swift fleeting pangs,
Sickening and deadly as a serpent's fangs.
Quivering in every limb then I was 'ware
Of a strange woman bending o'er me there,
With ashen hair, that in the moonlight pale
Rippled about her shoulders like a veil ;
In her cold eyes that pierced me through and
    through,
There dimly lurked a look that once I knew.
Her face was bloodless, as of one that 's dead,
But oh ! her little mouth, how rosy red,
Beset with glittering little fangs that bled,
Fresh from the cruel feast whereon they fed.
Cold was her bosom, and her clammy arms—
No ruddy current warmed those shapely charms.
The air grew stifling, and upon my ear
Fell strident whispers chilling me with fear.

" Dost thou not know my face ? in my close kiss
Lingers no essence of the olden bliss ?
5

Doth not my breath revive the ancient fire,
And fill the shrunken veins of dead desire?
I am the child of all thy joys; ere Death
Swallowed them up each left with me some breath,
Some drop of blood, some accent, or some look,
A token from each fleeting hour I took;
In me thy vanished raptures all unite
The perfect fruit of all thy past delight.
Long have I sought thee, now that thou art found,
Now that my limbs about thee have been wound,
And that my lips have fed upon thy face,
Nothing shall tear thee more from my embrace;
Dearer thou art to me than all that dwell
In the wide triple realms, Earth, Heaven and Hell.
Thou art my fruitful vineyard, and my well,
My gilded mountain top, and flowery dell
Whereon my lips shall pasture all the night,
Vanishing only with the morning light.
For in thy arms the olden joys I taste,
And round us swarm the spectres of the past;
The ruddy light still in their hollow eyes
Lingers that shone upon our revelries
In gay Lisboa's palaces of pride,
When every mask and cheek was flung aside,
Virtue was mocked, and God and man defied.

" And youthful joys far from Lisboa's town
Through some green byway of the years float
    down;

Over fair Lusitania's hills and plains
Again we wander free from sinful stains ;
Though viewed through mist of tears, the earliest
    scenes
Are brightest still whatever intervenes.
The leafy songs that thrill the listening wood,
And answering birds that make sweet interlude,
The sylvan lakes illuminated by
The rainbows arching all our summer sky,
And swans that drift along the shore at rest—
A string of pearls upon a swelling breast.''

Ranging amid the garden groves of youth,
The luring voice grew softer, till in sooth
Like pulsing of a moonlight lute it fell,
Lulling my senses with a rhythmic spell.
I know not if I slumbered, but anon
Those odious limbs about my own were thrown ;
I started up with thick and laboring breath,
And sickening loathing almost unto death ;
'' O Christ ! '' I cried, lo, at that sacred name
The foul shape vanished, and instead one came
Clad in soft light as from an inner flame,
And held an ebon cross whereon there bled
A great white Christ, with loving arms outspread.
Singing afar a tender voice I heard,
Faintly the accents fell, '' Flee as a bird.''
Then, as the spring-tides yearning to the moon,
Flood the dry hollows where we walked at noon,

E'en so the tidal-wave of feeling rose,
And memories wakened from their long repose,
And rushing back through many a dusty year
Left me again a reverent child at prayer.

Again the simple worshippers I saw
Kneeling in fervent prayer ; I heard with awe
Once more the shameful tale recounted o'er :
The buffets and revilings that He bore,
The crown of thorns, the wormwood, and the
    gall,
And our foul sins more bitter than them all,
Filling the cup that our vile hands have pressed
To the pure lips of our expiring Christ.
Gazing upon the Saviour's agony,
Through my dark soul a cleansing current swept,
And tears of humble penitence I wept.
Softly I wept at first, then gathering force,
Burst forth a storm of passionate remorse,
Till my frail couch shook like an autumn leaf
In the tempestuous torrent of my grief.
Stretching my trembling hands, "O Christ!" I
    cried,
"Would that with thee I might be crucified,
So I might share thy love.   O let me find
Some sure retreat remote from all my kind,
Far from the voice of priest or minister,
Where reigns the silence of the sepulchre ;
To some far rocky island let me flee,

Piercing the bosom of an unknown sea,
There let me live in sweet converse with thee.
Or in some Theban desert, too remote
E'en for the sound of Memnon's warning note,
Or 'mid the rocks on Sinai's shaking brow,
Where the fierce fires of God's anger glow ;
Or buried in some clammy convent cell,
No matter where, dear Lord, so I may dwell
Apart from all the universe but thee ;
So that my name may perish utterly
From memory of man ; so that no sound
Of human voice or footstep may resound
Through the deep portals of my solitude.
There let me purge my sins with penance rude,
The scourge, the midnight vigil, and the fast,
Until I know thee, face to face at last."
How weak are all this life's most tempting joys,
Love, wealth, ambition, transitory toys,
To those that flood the lonely anchorite
In the rapt moments of his soul's delight.
The sweetest words of Jesus are not found
In Holy Writ ; who in his grace abound,
Forsaking all the world to bear his cross,
Counting all human love and honor dross ;
Who wears the thorny crown upon his head,
And loveth better than his daily bread
The scourge, the iron chain, the stony bed,
Worn out with vigils, spent with sighs and tears,
Jesus perchance may whisper in his ears,

Sweeter than music of the choral spheres,
The unwritten words that soothed the Magdalene.
Perchance on Jesus' bosom he may lean,
A deeper sense than language can impart
Lies in the throbbing of that wondrous heart.

The moon went down, the night grew dark and
  dense,
The aspiration of my soul intense
Took real form and garb, or so it seemed,
And bore me on to all that I had dreamed.
Into the narrow dungeon where I lay
The Saviour came, and gently put away
My scourging hand ; his smile ineffable
With more than earthly radiance lit my cell—
Sweeter than wanton couch had ever known,
The rapture Jesus bringeth to his own.
Naked and prone upon the dungeon stone,
His love suffused me with a rosy glow.
His words of grace and pardon, murmured low,
Thrilled me and filled my spirit's pulsing vein,
Till like a ship impatient for the main
Her snowy wings tugged at the anchor chain.

I slept profoundly ; when I woke, the sun
Already more than half his course had run.
Light willing feet were moving round my couch,
And gentle hands with ministering touch.
They brought me dainties, and their cheerful
  words,

The hum of honey-bees, the voice of birds,
The grand old forest's potent influence
Subdued and mingled with my every sense,
And moved my being to accord and tune
With all the leafy harmonies of June,
As if some conscious hand beneficent
A hideous nightmare pall had from me rent.

I wandered out alone beneath the trees
And in a tempting spot reclined at ease,
My head in the cool shade, and at my feet
Streaming the amber sunlight's genial heat.
My spirits rose, and quickening pulses beat,
Surprised to find that living still was sweet.
The tree-tops o'er me seemed to melt away—
Green islets floating on an azure bay ;
And I in fancy floated with them, too,
Drifting forever down the ether blue.
Half dreaming thus, so quietly I lay
The forest denizens resumed their play ;
But furtively, as though they feared to break
The spell that brooded in the air, or wake
Some discord slumbering in the solitude.
A bird sang nigh me, but with voice subdued ;
The mossy oaks like kingly graybeards stood,
And stretched inviting arms ; the aspens wooed
With myriad beckoning leaves, and each slant
    beam,
Flung from the flying sun-god's hand, did seem

A rosy finger-tip that coyly pointed
To some deep trysting-place by wood-nymphs
    haunted.
Long vistas led away mysteriously,
So tempting that I almost thought to see
Arch faces from the nearer branches peeping,
And clumsy satyrs in the distance leaping.

The nymph, the satyr, and the bounding fawn
That filled the groves of Thessaly are gone.
The merry train that circled Oberon
Trip it no more upon the moonlit lawn.
But let them pass nor mourn the solitude :
Far sweeter than the whole fantastic brood
Is one weak, loving woman's human form.
A woman's voice, low, tremulous, and warm,
Hath a more potent spell to lull the charm
Than Orphean lute, or siren's song, where passed
The wave-worn mariner lashed to his mast.

Two doves thrust out their small heads timidly
From the low branches of a neighboring tree,
Looking askance, and peering through the green,
Like foolish lovers fearing to be seen,
Then, reassured, resumed their blissful play.
I smiled to see them, thinking of a day,
Just such another day as this, last year,
When with a damsel I had wandered here,
Amid these very vistas, and I thought

Of a deep vine-clad arbor we had sought.
Our words, our looks, our tender dalliance, all,
Like birds of passage at the swallow's call,
Came trooping back, on light wings fluttering,
And through me swept the quickening breath of
  spring.
Seen through the shimmering aspen leaves afar
A fair face twinkled on me like a star,
And rustle of bright garments drawing nigh
Fluttered my heart with strange expectancy.

.   .   .   .   .   .

And soon two happy lovers wandered far,
And tarried till the rising of the evening star.

TO ———.

HER heart is a flower that long hath slept
  Where clammy night-dews o'er it wept,
But now to love and rapture wakes
As the flushing glory of morning breaks,
And the heavy tears that chilled it so
Pure diamonds all in the sunshine glow.

Her hair is a sea of golden waves
Love's beauteous temple wall that laves,
Rippling o'er two rosy shells
Wherein the soul of music dwells,
To break in hyacinthine curl
Caressing the base of purest pearl.

Her eyes, twin mountain pools that lie
Reflecting back the summer sky,
A fringe of graceful poplars there
Sway softly in the amorous air.
Oh ! he who fathoms those wondrous eyes
Will see the joys of Paradise.

A crimson little rose her mouth
Exhales the memories of the South ;

74

And when its petals gently move,
Breathing some tender word of love,
No angel's voice at gates of bliss
Hath promise to compare with this.
Her brow a page of vellum fair,
'T were vain to seek for tracery there;
Pure as Mount Athos, yet I know
Beneath that alabaster brow
One tender secret, guarded well,
Stirs sweetly in its guarded cell.

. . . .

How many hundred hearts have beat
To the faint music of her feet ;
What yearning eyes devour the grass
That ripples where her footsteps pass,
Beneath her kirtle's airy sweep,
Like moonbeams glancing o'er the deep.

A snowy miracle of grace
Her circling arms, for whose embrace
Hyperion's self might vainly sigh.
Oh ! if within those arms to lie
To happy mortal e'er were given,
How tame were all the joys of heaven.
Sheltered by those endearing charms
From my own spirit's dark alarms,
Endymion were not half so blest
Fainting upon his Phœbe's breast.

TO ———.

REVOLVING years another May-day bring ;
  Earth at this bridal season's glad return
Blooms forth again in bridal robes of spring,
Expectant, waiting, trembling, all things yearn.
Cries then aloud the voice I thought was slain,
Calls as of yore my stormy deep to thine ;
Answer is mute, I hear no voice but mine.

TO THE SAME.

RARER and dearer seen through smiles or tears,
  Each day thy well-remembered face appears,
Beaming through all the clouds and mists of years.
Enfolding thee in dreams, my yearning kisses
Cling to that face till all our perished blisses
Come back like phantoms dear that re-awaken,
And haste to greet their loved ones long forsaken.

TO THE SAME.

RIGHT gladly would I twine a wreath of
  flowers,
Each morn for thee from dewy garden bowers ;
But when I cull them, lo ! they turn at view,
E'en in my hands, to nightshade and to rue ;
Circling, beloved one, thy temples rare,
Catching the halo of thy golden hair,
Again they glow, roses and lilies there.

TRANSLATIONS AND IMITATIONS

IF MY VERSES HAD WINGS LIKE A BIRD.

AFTER VICTOR HUGO.

IF my verses had wings like a bird,
   To thy garden of perfume and light
They would flutter with timid delight,
If my verses had wings like a bird.

If my verses, like fairies, had wings,
   To thy fireside at eve they would fly,
   To sparkle and gleam in thine eye,
If my verses, like fairies, had wings.

Pure pinions around and above,
   All day would rustle and gleam,
   They would whisper at night to thy dream,
If my verses were wingèd like Love.

'TWIXT SLEEP AND WAKING.

AFTER THE FRENCH OF PROSPER BLANCHEMAIN.

L YING alone last night, 'twixt sleep and
waking,
My cruel mistress passed, with queenly tread,
With smile of cold disdain, and haughty head,
And scornful eyes, whereat my heart was break-
ing;
The vision was so true in all its seeming,
I scarcely could believe that I was dreaming.

But when she came, and o'er me lowly bending,
Upon me rained the kisses of her mouth,
Laden with all the perfume of the South,
Murmuring the while of blisses never ending,
And in her eyes I saw the love-light gleaming,—
Ah! then I knew that I was only dreaming.

WHITE SWAN SAILING.

FROM THE RUSSIAN.

WHITE swan, sailing all the day,
  Peering in the wave below
As thou sailest proud and slow,
Round and round, and to and fro,
Seekest thou another, say?
Seest thou, in vaults below,
Through the wave inscrutable,
Joy of heaven or woe of hell?

Cruel swan, why mock me so?
Scornful sailing to and fro,
Answering not my questionings,
While above thy snowy breast
Rises haughty neck and crest.
Sure, beneath thy folded wings,
Knowledge lies of many things—
Secrets that I long to know.
Voices of the hollow wave,
Whispering as from a grave,
Murmur to thy listening ear
Secrets that I fain would hear.

Lo, I see another crest
Mirrored in the wave below,
And a bosom white as snow
Sails majestical and slow,
Unto thine 't is closely pressed ;
Face to face and breast to breast,
Two white swans majestic go
Round and round and to and fro.

Peering through the hollow wave
As into an open grave,
Lo, I see another there ;
Find the face and form of one,
Thought of whom I fain would shun
More than all beneath the sun ;
Find a face already where
Time's inexorable touch
Leaveth traces overmuch,
And steely fingers soon will tear,
Rending cruel furrows there.

Peering through the hollow wave,
Wistfully as in a grave,
Could I see another breast
As it was in Long Ago
(Or perhaps I dreamed it so),
Where my own might hope to rest ;
Not of mine the counterpart,
But a bosom white as snow,

Proud, but tender, pressed to mine,
As thy double unto thine ;
Would the rapture slay me, say?
Swelling, welling from my heart,
Soul and body rend apart?
Would the rapture slay me? nay,
Such a death were sweeter bliss
Than I find in life like this.

THE ROSES OF SAADI.

AFTER THE FRENCH OF DESBORDES-VALMORE.

A S I passed through the Valley of Roses to-day
    I gathered the fairest and sweetest for thee,
But my robes were so full that the knots burst
    away,
And all my sweet roses fell into the sea.

A wave slowly bore them away from my sight,
    Flaming forth like a cloud-billow rosy and red ;
But on me you may breathe all their fragrance to-
    night,
    For my bosom is sweet with the odors they
    shed.

ROSE-BUDS.

AFTER THE FRENCH OF BÉRANGER.

O TIMID rose-buds, why delay your bloom,
   The frost of Time is chill upon my hair ;
Unclose your petals, shed your sweet perfume,
Like vesper incense on the evening air.

Gladden my withered heart while yet you may,
   A rock is hid beneath each glowing wave ;
The ardent sun, wooing your lips to-day,
   To-morrow's noon may mock your poet's grave.

And rose-buds, ere their time may pass away ;
   The worm is there, an envious wind may
      blight ;
How many rose-buds have I seen decay,
   While thistles flaunt their colors in the light.

I pluck nor buds, nor full-blown roses now,
   Your tender charms from me have naught to
      fear ;
No rosy wreath awaits this wrinkled brow,
   Let regal youth the crown and sceptre bear.

85

Weary of strife, of cold, vain theorems,
  Of counting spots upon the sun's fair face,
Would that a bed beneath your friendly stems
  Were hollowed for my final resting-place.

When the Great Reaper comes, let me be found
  Among the roses, fresh and pure as truth ;
Their perfume shed above me and around,
  Whispering my failing heart of Love and
    Youth.

O timid rose-buds, why delay your bloom,
  The frost of Time is chill upon my hair ;
Unclose your petals, shed your sweet perfume
  Like vesper incense on the evening air.

THE BIRD I WAIT FOR.

AFTER THE FRENCH OF MOREAU.

D EAD, buried suns of former years arise,
And flowers bloom I thought had died last
  ` spring ;
The birds that fled last fall our wintry skies
  People again the woods on joyous wing ;
At dawn soft rustling pinions waken me,
  And swallows darken window-pane and door ;
Breathless I listen, gazing wistfully,
  Alas, the bird I wait for comes no more.

A high ambition swept my pulses through ;
  Gazing one day upon the eagle's flight,
I pierced with him the heaven's o'erarching blue,
  And beat my pinions at the gates of light.
To-day the bird of Jove alone defies
  The sun-god's burning glance, the tempest's
    roar ;
I watch his flight unmoved, with listless eyes,
  The bird I fondly wait for comes no more.

The lark pours forth his liquid flood of song,
   Seeking the secret covert where love lies,
Wherein to weave a palace for his young ;
   He sings his song, he loves his love and dies,
His sweet small soul with his own music thrilled.
   O mocking warbler, cease the song to pour,
Of Love victorious, fierce desire fulfilled,
   The bird I fondly wait for comes no more.

The martin hovers o'er the slumbering bay,
   Deep mirrored in the blue abyss he lies,
Now swiftly whirls and darts in idle play,
   Now rocked as in a poet's reveries.
O happy friend, follow thy fantasy,
   Dream on the wave, wanton along the shore,
The bird I fondly wait for comes no more.

Arrive at last, O messenger from heaven,
   Black envoy, bearing in thy beak of yore
The bread to famishing Elijah given.
   Has God for me no portion I implore ?
It soon will be too late, the shadows press,
   And night-birds gather round my darkening
      door.
Dead with the prophet in the wilderness,
   Alas, the bird I wait for comes no more.

VISIONS.

FROM THE FRENCH OF ALFRED DE MUSSET.

ONE midnight when I was a wayward child,
    I read by stealth a romance weird and wild ;
My veins were tingling and my cheeks aflame,
When suddenly before my vision came
Two sad dark eyes appealing wistfully,
A child in sable garb who looked like me.

A child so like to me in form and face,
It seemed a mirror standing in the place.
He cast on me one long and earnest look,
Then bent with me o'er the forbidden book.
A smile mysterious he wore, but never spoke,
And vanished from me as the daylight broke.

The years sped by ; one dreamy autumn day
The eager chase had led me far astray ;
Fantastic shadows thronged the solitude
Of the deep mountain forest where I stood,
And there appeared beneath a spreading tree,
A wanderer dressed in black, who looked like me.

He held a quaint old lute and a fresh spray
Of eglantine ; I gently asked my way.

He answered me no word, but took with pride
A path straight up the towering mountain side.
His parting glance fell on me with a thrill
Of meaning so intense it haunts me still.

Another year sped by ; one night outside
The room wherein my sainted mother died
I stood alone, and friendless with my grief—
Youth's crushing grief that hopes not for relief,—
I oped the door, lo, there on bended knee
An orphan dressed in black who looked like me.

Kneeling before the sacred ashes there
He seemed a radiant angel in despair.
His face was bathed in tears, his head was crowned
With thorns, his lute was flung upon the ground,
And o'er his sable garments flowed a tide
Of crimson from the sword that pierced his side.

Since then in every crisis I have known,
Whether in busy town or desert lone,
Angel or demon, whichsoe'er it be,
That sable apparition comes to me.
I never hear his voice, he stands apart,
Yet like a brother twines about my heart.

Now, all my idols burned in civil strife,
Willing to love or re-create my life,
My feet, self-exiled from their natal strand,
Gather the dust of many a foreign land ;

A labyrinthine maze I vainly grope,
Seeking the faint, vague vestige of a hope.

Still in those moments when life's pulses go
Surging almost to fatal overflow,
When the blind, fettered spirit seems at last
Ready its fetters and its scales to cast,
Before my vision comes, on land or sea,
A wanderer, dressed in black, who looks like me.

THE FISHERMAN'S BRIDAL.

AFTER DELAVIGNE.

THE sea is high, the night is dark,
  Sweet son, O why unmoor thy bark
Before the morning ?
On such a night as this last year,
I fain had kept thy brother here ;
  O heed the warning.
      But the fisherman smiling
        Bounded from shore,
      His labor beguiling,
        Bending the oar,
      Singing, she loveth me,
        No fear I know,
      No wave appalleth me,
        Loving her so.

With white wing cleft the inky sky,
A sea-bird with a plaintive cry,
    Saddening the air :
The nest I built with so much toil,
This night became the tempest's spoil ;
    Beware, beware !

Still the fisherman smiling,
Bending the oar,
The darkness beguiling,
Sang as before:
My Nanna calleth me,
No fear I know,
No wave appalleth me,
Loving her so.

Faintly arose a sad appeal,
Blent with the storm by which his keel
Was rudely driven.
O brother, ere thy knell shall toll,
Pray for thy elder brother's soul,
Who died unshriven.
But the message unheeded
Its warning bore,
As onward he speeded,
Bending the oar,
Murmuring, she calleth me,
No fear I know,
No wave appalleth me,
Loving her so.

Weary at dawn he reached the strand,
But lo, there passed a mourning band;
For whom? he cried.
For whom, O fishermen, that bell
That strikes upon my heart its knell?
'T is for thy bride.

Then as if on the shore,
  Stricken down by a dart,
Deep darkness came o'er
  Him, chilling his heart,
Whispering, she calleth me,
  No fear I know,
No wave appalleth me,
  Loving her so.

YOU HAD MY WHOLE HEART.

FROM THE FRENCH OF DESBORDES VALMORE.

Y OU had my whole heart,
I thought I had thine,
No beguiling or art,
A heart for a heart.

Your heart is returned,
But alas ! where is mine ?
Your heart is returned,
But mine you have spurned.

The leaf and the bloom
And the fruit of the same,
Leaf, color, and bloom,
Sweet flower and perfume.

Oh, what hast thou done ?
My sovereign supreme,
Oh, what hast thou done ?
Beneath the fair sun.

An orphan bereft
Of mother and home,
An orphan bereft,
With my grief I am left.

Deserted, alone,
Through the cold world to roam,
Deserted, alone,
But heaven hears my moan.

One day you will muse,
Broken-hearted and old,
One day you will muse
On the love you refuse.

You will seek me one day
But you shall not behold ;
You will call me one day,
I shall not obey.

You will come to my door
With penitent head,
A friend, as of yore,
You will knock at my door.

It will coldly be said,
She is gone, she is dead ;
Her spirit has fled,
Will coldly be said.

ART.

FROM THE FRENCH OF THÉOPHILE GAUTIER.

YES, art with grievous pangs is born
    From Nature's most endearing molds ;
        The child is torn,
Not wooed, from fierce rebellious folds.

Slay not thy art by false constraint,
    Yet know her rules are stern as Fate ;
        Without complaint
The muse should wear a buskin strait.

Would'st have thy verse endure, thy muse
    The common facile forms must shun,
        The slipshod shoes
In which so many feet have run.

Sculptor, beware the plastic clay,
    Changing at every whim's command
        From day to day,
And marred by every careless hand.

Strive with the marbles pure of Greece,
    Wrested from Paros' snowy mines,
        Smite, and release
The deep-imprisoned god-like lines.

The chisel of Praxiteles
  Such peerless beauty had not known,
    If art in Greece
  Had deigned to use a meaner stone.

Let the fierce molten metal fuse
  Heroic forms and high contours
    Of Syracuse ;
Nought but the matchless bronze endures.

Upon the agate's flinty face
  Apollo's features high and pure
    In profile trace,
With touches delicate and sure.

Beware of water and pastel,
  Deep on fantastic vase and urn
    Thy colors frail
In seven-fold heated furnace burn.

Fashion the writhing, maddening limb
  Of nymph and goddess ; bring once more
    The monsters grim,
Dear to the blazonry of yore.

The virgin mother saintly mild,
  Crowned with her nimbus ; on her breast
    The wondrous child,
The globe beneath the cross of Christ.

Crowns fall and sceptres pass, robust
  And radiant art outlives them all.
    Torso and bust
  Survive the city's triple wall.

The medal by the ploughman found
  Reveals the countenance austere,
    The temples crowned,
  That filled the antique world with fear.

Even the gods wax old and pass
  From high Olympus ; verse alone,
    Stronger than brass,
  Preserves to fallen Zeus his throne.

The graver guide with care supreme,
  The chisel smite, fix like a rock
    Thy floating dream
  Deep in the stern resisting block.

Tongues and religions die, while art,
  Poised in the lofty realms of thought,
    Serene, apart,
  Exults in sempiternal youth.

BARCAROLLE.

FROM THE SAME.

O SUN-BRIGHT maiden, choose and say,
 Whither shall we two sail to-day ?
The rose's breath is on the gale
That softly moves our silken sail ;
Our masts of gleaming ivory
 Are strung like harps with yellow hair,
 That make Æolian music there ;
A seraph shall our pilot be.

O sun-bright maiden, choose and say,
Whither shall we two sail to-day ?
Our pinnace lifts her snowy wing
And flutters like a living thing ;
And from the shore the morning wind
 Toys with our awning's purple fold ;
 Our rudder is of beaten gold
And leaves a rosy track behind.

O sun-bright maiden, choose and say,
Whither shall we two sail to-day ?

Our hold with love-apples is stored,
And all strange fruits, a goodly hoard ;
A wingèd boy sits at the prow,
　Pointing our path with beaming eye
　And smile of deepest mystery ;
A wreath of myrtle crowns his brow.

O sun-bright maiden, choose and say,
Whither in Love's realm shall we stray ?
Say, shall we seek some storied isle,
Where warm Ægean waters smile?
Or shall I see the Arctic sun
　A flood of crimson glories shed
　At midnight on that golden head,
Or sail to seas where pearls are won ?

O sun-bright maiden, choose and say
Whither shall we two sail to-day ?
Follow the track of Heracles—
Seeking the far Hesperides ;
Or where the South Sea flower expands,
　Float idly in the moonlight wan ;
　Or sail beneath the rainbow's span—
Bright gateway to Love's golden lands?

O sun-bright maiden, choose and say,
There is no one to say thee nay.
O seek, she saith, that faithful shore
Where loving hearts will change no more.

Alas, my sails for many a year
  Have sped through all Love's wide domain,
  Seeking that blessed shore in vain :
That land is still unknown, my dear.

SHADOWS.

FROM THE SAME.

BE still, my heart, keep silence, O my soul,
  Thy fierce rebellious transports are in vain,
Oblivion's turbid wave must o'er thee roll.

Cease the faint pulsing of the weary brain,
Fold up the remnant of thy wings at last,
And rot, beneath the inexorable chain.

Soon shalt thou be with refuse vile outcast,
Flung down the bottomless abyss that still
Yawns to the future from the darkling past.

Thy hopes are dead, broken thy lofty will,
Thy name and memory will be blotted out
Before the rattling clods thy grave refill.

No marble shaft for thee the heavens will flout,
Nor tear-drenched willow shed her graceful spray,
No lying epitaph the truth will scout,

No choir will chant, no man of God will pray,
No tears will silver the funereal pall—
Dark cloud that hides thy shame from light of day.

The felled tree strangely moves his comrades tall,
Waking the echoes of the mountain side,
But not a leaf will quiver at thy fall.

Like the mute convoy of the suicide,
Thou shalt wind down through night to find thy
    doom :
Thy ashes shall be scattered far and wide.

No circling rings shall break the sullen gloom
Of the dark pool that closes o'er thy head,
No widowed soul shall hover o'er thy tomb.

For the chaste secrets which thy soul hath wed,
With thee the pit shall bury them from view,
Fathoms below the deepest deep-sea lead.

Our Mother, Nature, hath her favorites too,
Like any other dame, spoiled children they ;
Unwelcome waif, why should they share with
    you ?

Upon them fall the myrtle and the bay,
E'en in the desert they would find at need
Enchanted palaces along their way.

Though for the morrow's morn they take no
    heed,
Yet through their fingers filter golden sands,
And at a generous breast they freely feed.

Kneading a withered breast with famished hands
Their outcast brethren pine, or seek in vain
Some kinder bosom in relentless lands.

And if for them upon the desert plain
Illusive gardens rise, and fountains play,
They vanish like the rainbow after rain.

Or if by chance a sunbeam gone astray
Glints through the gloom that shrouds them ever-
    more,
A chilling cloud obscures th' unwonted ray.

The wisest plans but mock their hopes the more,
Bringing them to derision and dismay :
The sea engulfs them though they hug the shore.

The tree shall crush them, hollow with decay,
Whose grateful shade invites them to draw nigh :
The heart they lean on wins them to betray.

A turtle drops upon them from the sky ;
The tower that has braved a thousand years
Falls without warning just as they pass by.

The friend who shared their youthful smiles and
    tears
Accuses them of treason to the crown,
Sending them to the rack with blows and jeers.

Born on the Danube, in the Seine they drown ;
Poor fools, why fly so far to find the fate
That like a slimy monster sucks them down ?

Why strive with Fate ? no jot will he abate ;
Even the brawny knees of Hercules
Must bend or break before him soon or late.

They drain a bitter cup with poisonous lees,
A life ignoble and a death of shame,
And in some potter's field they find surcease ;

Or, dying nobly, leave behind no name,
While, mounting on their bones, some brazen
    cheat
Reaches the very pinnacle of Fame.

Destiny mocks them from her lofty seat,
Dipping their sponge in vinegar and gall :
Want grinds them in the dust with iron feet.

Hard by the accursed sea whose waves appal,
A scape-goat lone, beneath the wingless skies,
They wander where the ashen apples fall.

Night takes for them a thousand baleful eyes,
Piercing at once their deepest hiding-place :
Straight to their heart each poisoned arrow flies.

Thrust out of camp, the scape-goat of their race,
Abhorred they live, and dead, the loathing earth
Vomits their phantom from the burial-place.

Such is thy history, O my soul, from birth ;
Dark pages with decaying odors rife,
A maze of treachery, and pain, and dearth.

Yet 't is the story of a vulgar life ;
No title casts a glamour o'er its woes,
No footlights gild its unromantic strife.

Across the web the flying shuttle goes,
Weaving with common threads a homely plot,
Yet dark and sinister the pattern shows.

Why woo so long a world that loves thee not ?
O soul, whence long have perished hope and
    faith,
Why cling to life, when death is all thy lot ?

Sweeter than bridal bed the couch of death,
More restful far than sleep ; the asphodel
Is sweeter than the crimson poppy's breath.

King, queen, and harlot, priest and infidel,
Heaped up at random peacefully they rest,
Commingling in one mighty urn pell-mell.

Despairing brother, whose fast chilling breast
Nor love, nor wine may warm, descend with me,
And burst the shadowy gates an eager guest.

Abase thy head, and bend thy stubborn knee ;
And like a Scythian chief in triumph led,
Welcome the agony that sets thee free.

One short, fierce agony, and all is said ;
Beneath the coffin lid, sealed once for all,
Compose thy limbs as in a royal bed.

Swift as the fleeting shadow on the wall
Thy feeble footprints fall along the sand,
Nor voice, nor echo will thy song recall.

In the Corinthian brass thy feeble hand
Can write no name ; thy chisel cannot bite
The marbles of Carrara pure and grand.

He who would climb Fame's towering mountain
    height
Must have a double gift, a genius rare :
Unto a happy star he must unite.

Poet, alas ! and lover, brethren are ;
Twins of the soul, each hath his cherished dream,
Some saint ideal, worshipped from afar ;

Some fount of youth, some pure Pactolian stream,
Some orb that beams with strange unearthly ray,
Some flaming vision potent to redeem.

The fount is dry, the vision fades away ;
The mystic light that led them through the night
Dies in a marsh, and leaves them far astray.

O God, to tread but once by morning light
The alabaster palace of our dreams,
Counting its colonnades with waking sight ;

To greet the lovely images that gleam
Athwart the gardens of our revery,
And drink the waters of its mystic stream ;

To make the plunge, piercing triumphantly
The crystal vault, bring back the golden vase
Long buried with the treasures of the sea.

'T were fine to feel the thrill of flight through
    space,
Adown the far empyrean to float,
Or track the eagle in his headlong chase.

To find the deed outstrip the noble thought,
To find fit words to mate our passion's cry,
And pour the tide with its full burden fraught.

Sailing through unknown seas, to catch the sigh
Of mighty rivers, and through night's eclipse
See new worlds heaving upward to the sky;

To feel upon the flower of our lips
The regal kiss that sometimes hovers there;
To find the glen wherein the rainbow dips;

To stop the wheel of fortune in the air;
To see before us on the glowing page
The wavering thoughts our midnight musings
　　bear.

Such lots, alas, in this decrepit age
Are rare; Polycrates might wear his ring,
Nor fear to rouse the avenging goddess' rage.

Seeking the upper chambers where we cling,
The cruel wave mounts upward step by step,
Mingling its murmur with our revelling,

Till slimy phocas, shapes that banish sleep,
Gnash foully at our very bedsides there,
Belched from the bowels of the nether deep.

The church is dark, the altar cold and bare,
And rending from their brows the aureole,
The saints blaspheming die in their despair.

The sun senescent, near his final goal,
Casts from his bloodshot eye one baleful glare,
Ere yet the heavens vanish like a scroll.

Each living thing shall perish foul or fair,
The flood will top the tallest mountain chain,
For vengeance cometh on and will not spare.

For twenty days and nights through wind and
    rain,
The raven's midnight wing, cleaving the waste,
Seeks for a haven where to rest in vain.

Headlong she falls, famished and spent at last,
And as the widening circles mark the flood,
All Earth is but a tomb whence life has passed.

A common sepulchre for bad and good,
Upon this wave no ark of safety rides,
Bitter with tears and red with human blood.

No second patriarch his vessel guides,
A hive of life ; a swelling fountain head,
To burst upon Ararat's rugged sides.

Atlas has fallen ! hark, O hark ! o'erhead
The crack of doom, the supports of the world
Are snapped like reeds beneath Behemoth's tread.

Our Mother Earth, by storms of chaos whirled,
Reels like a drunken harlot down through space,
By wanton buffets from her orbit hurled.

Unto the lips of an expiring race
The Son holds up the cup of human woes;
The Father sees with coldly sneering face.

When will our crucifixion cease? still flows
The ruddy current from our open side,
And red drops cluster on our pallid brows.

Enough of tears and blood; O turn aside
The poisoned chalice; doth not this suffice?
That Thy dear Son upon the cross has died?

He died for naught; man still must pay the price
Unless a newer Christ rise from the dead:
The Pontiff asks a fresher sacrifice.

For nigh two thousand years the Lamb hath bled;
His empty veins leave not the faintest stain
Upon the priestly knife that gleams o'erhead.

Messiah cometh not, we watch in vain;
The vail is rent, broken the altar stone,
The worshippers are slain, the church o'erthrown.

SONNET : *OU VONT ILS ?*

FROM THE FRENCH OF SULLY PRUDHOMME.

TO what strange land gather the slain of Love ?
　Heaven were no world for them, it hath no
　　bliss
To match the raptures that they knew in this ;
No summer night, no dark secluded grove,
Or deep ravine with sheltering boughs above ;
　Nor can the foul fiends of the dread abyss
　So rend a soul as the fierce agonies
Of Love's disdain, the doubts and fears thereof.

Tame were the joys of the bright sphere above
　To which the saints so ardently aspire,
　And vain the anguish of eternal fire
To him who knows the martyrdom of Love.
For souls consumed and dead there is no room
In heaven or hell : oblivion is their doom.

THE GAY CASHIER.

ADAPTED FROM THE FRENCH.

TWO gallant burglars, who for many a day
   Had laid their plans, at last had made their
      way
Into a bank upon a stormy night;
Then with what fond, what rapturous delight
Unto the vault they flew to seize the swag !
   O cruel joke, there was no swag at all :
That night the gay cashier, a heartless wag,
   With all the funds had skipped for Montreal.

THE RAVAGES OF TIME.

SCARRON.

THE monuments of human pride and power,
Engulfed by ocean wave or desert sand,
And crushed by time's inexorable hand,
Built for eternity, last but an hour.
Where are the hanging gardens and the towers
Of Babylon? the marbles tall and grand
That stood like gods on the Ægean strand?
Fallen and crumbled. So shall crumble ours.

Time slays or withers all on which we dote;
His swift, remorseless touches ne'er relent,
Destroying marble, mortar, and cement.
Then why should I repine because my coat
Is threadbare on the seams with three years' wear,
Out at the elbows, and beyond repair?

HALLUCINATION.

FROM THE FRENCH.

I.

L AST night, or did I dream ? my lady led
    Me to a wall I oft had passed before,
  And opened there a curious secret door
Made by some cunning workmen ages dead.
We entered furtively, and as our tread
    Resounded on the long untrodden floor,
    Back swung the portal with a clanging roar.
Fleeing like startled children on we sped,
And found an inner chamber, where was spread
    A board with gold and crystal, and a store
    Of fruits and flowers from every unknown
        shore,
And curious flasks, whose contents gleaming red
A ruddy radiance o'er my lady shed,
    And flung fantastic flames upon the floor.

116

II.

Bathed in the amber of an unseen flame,
  A royal couch with silken curtains fair
Gleamed like a jewel in the alcove there ;
A dreamy languor stole through all my frame,
  Sweet beyond power of language to declare ;
  A breath of perfume moved the swooning air,
Stirring the golden ringlets of my dame ;
And while we faltered, lo, a small voice came :
"O happy pair, with rosy forms aglow,
Here lie within the temple's deep alcove
Sweet mysteries that I pant to have you know ;
Wine that hath stained the trampling feet of Love,
And fruit that ripened in the sacred grove :
Break every seal, and let the purple flow."

III.

I turned to seek my lady's eyes, when lo !
  The vision vanished, and I stood alone
  Without the temple walls, whose cold gray
    stone
Mocked my endeavor, rising row on row.
I called my lady's name, fearful and low.
  No answer, save the hoot-owl's jeering tone,
  And the pale mocking moon that coldly shone.
Now, sadly round the temple walls I go,
Whose deepest mysteries I thought to know.

I thought its inmost chamber mine ; fond fool,
I only stood within some vestibule,
Where all men's feet may wander to and fro,
And saw, reflected from some mirror there,
My own imaginings too warm and fair.

IV.

IN THE GROVE.

Once more the huntress clad in silvery mail
    Seeks her Endymion, over hill and glade ;
    Once more the hour so dear to youth and maid—
The hour that all Love's guardian spirits hail.
Wrapped in the moonlight like a lucent veil,
    Is it for me, young priestess, that, arrayed
    Still in thy vestal robes, thy feet have strayed
So far from where the sacred fires pale ?

Last night within the temple's dim alcove
    I durst not lift my conscious eyes to thine.
    Lo, now thy lips and eyes have sought for mine,
    And round my neck thy sheltering arms en-
        twine,
While our commingling footsteps freely rove
Through all the mysteries of the silent grove.

TO MY CRITICS.

IMITATED FROM DE MUSSET.

M Y verse contains some images, 't is true,
On Byron's pages found, what then, he too
On other pages found them long before,
(Byron, I think, would hardly grudge them me,
Seeing I need them so much worse than he).
Read carefully the old Italian lore,
If you, to draw it very mild, would see
How freely Byron borrowed ; he or she
As stupid as a school teacher must be
Who thinks in eighteen hundred eighty-four
To find a thought or rhyme not used before.
And yet I must not speak of " waters blue,"
Of " sunny skies," and " eyes of heavenly
hue,"
Nor use some old stock metaphor at need
Because, forsooth, pedantic fools may read
The same in every language,—Sanscrit, Greek,
Hebrew and Latin, Dutch and Arabic.
Great bards of yore, and they of yesterday,
Before whose sun my rushlight pales away,
To whose deep flood, my song is but a rill,—
All, great and small, hear the same chorus still.

Read the old rotting magazines and see
The very venom that they void on me ;
The arsenal where roving malice meets
The rusty darts that stung the heart of Keats.
Vile innuendo, and malignant sneer,
Blanche, Tray, and Sweetheart, hardly changed
      are here.

The lowest place amid the minstrel throng
Is all I claim ; in the full tide of song
My voice is lost ; upon my page appears
No burning message from supernal spheres.
But Teian glow and Lesbian passion still
A thousand lyres in every land they thrill.
A chord once found belongs, the whole world
      through,
To every minstrel that can strike it true.
My verses rhyme (at least some of them do),
And sweet as ever in our ear there chimes
The melody of old recurrent rhymes.
Dove ever mates with love, and bliss with kiss,
In every song from Sappho's day to this.

THE YOUTH AND THE OLD MAN.

FLORIAN.

" OLD man," said an ambitious youth one
    day,
" Show me the path to wealth and fame, I pray."
Answering not, the old man mused awhile,
His thin lips wreathing with a cynic smile,
Then spoke : " Is fame thy wish ? With earnest
    zeal
Devote thyself to serve the commonweal ;
To her give all thy talents and thy time,
The flush of youth, and vigorous manhood's prime;
And should the foeman come with deadly strife,
In her defence be swift to lose thy life,
Perchance with ' failure ' branded on thy heart.
The road to wealth is surer ; seek the mart,
Where cunning money-changers lie in wait,
Casting their nets with watered stocks for bait.
Or join the nobler throng, whose argosies
Bear on white wings across the distant seas
The honest——" " Hold, old man, I 'll none of
    these ;

With intrigue and deceit I would not soil
My soul, and yet I shrink from sordid toil."

Again the old man mused in silence while
Around his mouth hovered a cynic smile,
Then answered thus : " Why, simply be a fool,
And win both fame and wealth, in spite of rule."

THE CATHEDRAL BELL AND ITS RIVAL.

IRIARTE.

IN a renowned cathedral hung a bell,
   The pride of all the country far and near ;
A bell whose deep vibrations never fell
   Save on the greatest church-days of the year.
Then for some moments brief the air was thrilled
   By some deep strokes with solemn pause be-
      tween ;
The heart devout with pious awe was filled,
   And sinners felt repentance swift and keen.

Within a neighboring hamlet poor and small,
With crumbling belfry tottering to its fall,
There stood a paltry chapel low and mean ;
A cracked and rusty cow-bell hung therein,

Harsh and discordant, but the sexton sly,
Only upon the solemn days and high,
Six times a year at most, its voice awoke,
Like the cathedral bell with solemn stroke.
This strange reserve, in parish bells unknown,
Gave to the wretched bell a high renown.

Its jangling equalled to the rustic's ear
The tones majestic of its grand compeer.

Pretentious, owl-like silence oft supplies
The lack of wit in those accounted wise.
" Be swift to listen and be slow to speak,"
If a high name for wisdom you would seek.

BLUE EYES AND BLACK EYES.

IMITATED FROM ANDALUSIAN COPLAS.

I.

TWO miracles are thy blue eyes,
　　Haughty or tender ;
Robbing our Andalusian skies
　　Of half their splendor.

Celestial eyes of heaven's own hue,
　　Twin thrones of glory,
Whose glances every day subdue
　　New territory.

Blue were the waters and the skies
　　Of happy Eden ;
And blue should be a Christian's eyes,
　　Matron or maiden.

By heaven those peerless orbs of blue
　　To thee were given,
And all the mischief that they do
　　Is known in heaven.

I thought thy blue eyes beacons fair,—
    O treacherous seeming ;
O treacherous waves of golden hair,
    That wrecked my dreaming !

Two saints the blue eyes seemed to me
    That wrought my ruin :
Who would have thought that saints could be
    A soul's undoing ?

II.

Black eyes are truer still, I ween,
    Than any other :
Dark were the eyes of Eden's Queen,
    And Mary Mother.

The holy ones of sacred lore
    All dark are painted,
Inspired prophetess of yore
    And maiden sainted.

Blue eyes are cold as polished steel,
    For all their splendor ;
While thine a lambent flame reveal,
    So warm and tender.

Dearer thine olive hue, and eyes
  Of raven blackness,
Than all the azure of the skies,
  And lily's whiteness.

Thine eyebrows are a Moorish grove,
  Whence issuing fleetly
Two wingèd archers lightly rove,
  Wounding so sweetly.

But when their victims bleeding lie
  Faintly appealing,
Two tender blackamoors draw nigh
  With balm of healing.

COMPLAINT TO THE VIRGIN.

FROM A CUBAN POETESS.

MOTHER ineffable, whose radiant brow
    The stars have crowned,
O'er all earth's daughters chosen, thou
    The sinless found ;

Of Adam's fallen race, the first and last
    Untouched by strife,
Whose beauteous feet unstained and pure have
    passed
    The snares of life.

The angelic heralds at those spotless feet
    Once bent the knee,
And now adore at the effulgent seat
    Eternally.

A gift too pure and bright for earthly bloom,
    Flower of the sky ;
The odors of whose matchless grace perfume
    The courts on high.

Look down in pity from thy lofty throne,
    Through realms of light,
To where thy sorrowing sister walks alone
    In deepest night.

Oh, see the endless waves of anguish fierce
    That o'er me roll !
Hast thou not bled ? did not the sword once pierce
    Thy tender soul ?

Beating the breakers on the outer bar
    My vessel lies ;
For me there beams no friendly guiding-star,
    No beacons rise.

Blest beacon seen in my despairing dreams,
    Burst forth on me,
And light my stormy pathway with thy beams,
    Star of the sea.

O baleful night, when some malignant blast,
    Mocking and wild,
Into an orphan's cradle rudely cast
    A sleeping child !

Of careless childhood's flowers and smiles and
    tears,
    The tears were mine.
Alas ! I gather in maturer years
    No fruit or wine.

9

All night I bruise my failing wings in vain,
    Seeking for rest—
A bird unmated on an arid plain
    Without a nest.

I roam a timid stranger on the earth—
    A foreign land—
Bewildered by the light, the joy and mirth
    On every hand.

A vine-clad mountain to the beaming skies
    That lifts its crest,
While an abyss of untold horror lies
    Beneath its breast.

Some loving souls at birth are consecrated
    To pain and grief;
Through gloomy vales they stray, unknown, un-
    mated,
    Without relief.

I seek no longer these sad mysteries
    To penetrate ;
I must not murmur at the high decrees
    That fix my fate.

They say that God regards with pitying eye
    The poor and weak,
Smiting the haughty head, and passing by
    The low and meek.

No daring oak, whose branches, heaven defying,
    Pierce the blue sky ;
A blighted leaf before the tempest flying,
    A reed am I.

A poor blind pilgrim through the wilderness
    Groping my way,
Striving with agonizing tears to press
    From night to day.

A heart whence all illusions long have perished
    Seeks not for bliss.
I ask not human love, O Mother cherished,
    I ask but this :

A lowly shelter far from tongues maligning
    And bitter sneers ;
There let me pray and quench all fierce repining
    With grateful tears.

And some glad morning through my cloister
    swelling,
    A golden portal
May burst, and flood with rosy light my dwelling,
    And joys immortal.
Q

THE CRUCIFIXION.

OLD FRENCH SONNET.

WHILE Jesus suffered for the human race
    Upon the tree, death came and found him
      there.
  Transfixed with shame, at first he did not dare
To look upon his sovereign's awful face.

But Jesus, full of majesty and grace,
    Meekly bowed down his head, august and fair,
    Veiling the glory that it used to wear,
And waves of darkness fell upon the place.

Then shuddering Death his shameful task ful-
    filled;
    Earth to her centre rocked as though the day
    Of doom were come; the veil was rent away—
All Nature moaned and quivered, horror-filled.

The very stones were softened, thou alone,
Vile scoffing sinner, took a heart of stone.

FROM THE SPANISH.

UNHAPPY he who buys
   The toys that Cupid offers ;
For each delight he proffers
Some dear illusion dies.
Sell not thy dearest treasures
For his too fleeting pleasures.

THE BOOK OF LIFE.

LAMARTINE.

E ACH soul the Book of Life must read and
  prove—
Fate turns the leaves whether we will or no.
We cannot linger o'er the lines we love,
  Or hasten o'er the dreary lines of woe.
We have not read the page of Love aright
When, lo ! the page of Death appalls our sight.

MEMORIAL DAY, AND OTHER POEMS.

TWENTY YEARS AGO.

WRITTEN FOR MEMORIAL DAY IN 1885.

FOR twenty years the snowy wings of Peace
Over the land have brooded ; flocks increase
Upon the fields, now blessed by smiling stars,
Where drave the reeking chariot-wheels of Mars.
How like a falcon's flight the years have flown,
Since Appomattox rang the curtain down ;
And listening to my voice are tall young men,
And women fair who were but children then.
Our young Republic, freed from all his chains,
For peaceful conquest girds his lusty reins.
The smiling Mississippi to the sea
Rolls as in days of old, unvexed and free,
And East and West in one grand commonweal
Are bound by triple bands of shining steel.
The apple tree historic rots away ;
Our gunboats all have crumbled to decay ;
The rifle-pits that scarred the Southern plains
Are washed away by twenty winters' rains ;
The impetuous onset of the bayonet line
Tramples no more the growing corn and vine,
And nesting birds pour forth their raptures where
The thunder-bolts of battle rent the air.

But still remain in many hearts we know
The ghastly scars of twenty years ago.
How many a comrade's widow treads alone
A narrow path by cruel thorns o'ergrown !
'T is long since song of mating bird has thrilled
That lonely heart, with tender memories filled,—
Memories still speeding backward to the time
When, brave and beautiful in manhood's prime,
Her bridegroom more than twenty years ago
Sprang at the bugle call to meet the foe.
Strong men for other women dig the gold,
Tread out the wine, and weave the silken fold ;
Her wine of Life in forests dark and dank
The thirsty soil of Mississippi drank ;
Her daily lot for more than twenty years
Has been the widow's toil, and widow's tears.

Comrades, we 're growing old ; upon our hairs
Gather the frosts of more than twenty years,
Since in the trench at Petersburg we lay,
Or, gayly holding our triumphal way,
Unto the sea we swept with Sherman's pennon,
Or heard the roar of Stonewall Jackson's cannon,
Waking the echoes of the Rapidan,
Or through the valley whirled with Sheridan.
Still surges up as though of yesterday
The memory of those that passed away ;
Still floating down the vista of the years,
We hear their voices, see their smiles and tears.

In each successive strife how fast they fell—
The tried companions that we knew so well.
Some, fleeing from the ghastly prison pen,
By bloodhounds tracked were slain in swamp and
      fen ;
Some ashes mingle with the sounding tide,
And some enrich the rugged mountain side,
Where the tall pines of frowning Kenesaw
Quivered like reeds before the blast of war ;
Now looming up in shadowy ranks they stand
Like guardian phantoms brooding o'er the land.
No higher impulse thrilled the knights of old
Who to the crusades like a torrent rolled,
To pour for the dear cross their blood like wine
Upon the plains of Holy Palestine,
And feed on desert sands in the far East
The jackals ravening for their glorious feast.

They reck not where their scattered ashes rest
Who speed to the reunion of the blest ;
As eaglets soaring to the gates of light
Spurn the dull shells that long confined their
      flight.
For you the amaranthine wreath we twine,
Raise the high song, and pour the ruddy wine ;
For you the rhythmic beat of martial feet,
As the long lines go swaying down the street ;
For you the plantive reed's subduing moan
Commingles with the hautboy's rapturous tone,

The rolling drum, the thrilling trumpet blare,
And silken banners float upon the air
Like bright ethereal drapery trailing there.
The noblest sons of Earth, of every clime,
Welcome you to their galaxy sublime ;
And flowers, by maidens fairer still than they,
Are offered to your sacred shades to-day ;
Roses and dittany—and lilies fair,
Mingle their breath upon the vernal air ;
But sweeter than the fleeting gifts we bring
Your memory perennial shall spring,
And loving tears each spring-time shall bedew
The flowers that loving hands shall here renew ;
And younger bards, with truer touch than mine,
Will pour for you the flood of song divine,
While millions yet unborn, with quickening
    breath,
Will hear the tale heroic of your death.

O host of gallant comrades sweeping by,
Up the red track of glory to the sky—
Reynolds, McPherson, Dahlgren, Garesché,
And all the unknown names as brave as they,—
Great hearts and souls as those of song and story,
Whose only guerdon was a deathbed gory ;
As youthful as of yore we see you now,
The flush of victory on each radiant brow,
And youthful in our withering hearts shall glow
Your generous valor in the Long Ago.

ABRAHAM LINCOLN.

SONG, legend, history, I scan in vain ;
    Outside of Holy Writ, no shape appears
  So godlike as thy homely form ; the spheres
Darken and die, thy glory shall not wane.
Monarchs have sat self-crowned upon the Seine
    And on the Tiber ; nations sick with fears
    Have builded altars to them, drenched with tears
And smoking with a hecatomb of slain.

O Christ of Freedom, no high altars fume
    For thee, but freely flow the tears and blood,
The pure sweet blood of thy own martyrdom,
    And tears of mingled grief and gratitude
From the dark millions by thy pen set free,
Led from their long Gethsemane by thee.

THE PRISONER'S DREAM.

ON the last sad day of the dying year,
  As I lay in my prison racked with pain,
I heard the voices of children clear
  Swelling out on the night in a peaceful strain.
They sang a farewell to the dying year,
  And the far faint tones of an organ fell
With a soothing cadence upon my ear,
  And I slept at last in my loathsome cell.
My body slept with its clanking chain, ·
  But the prison walls fled far away,
And my spirit, glad and free again,
  Went forth as upon its bridal day.
I never had thought again to sing,
  But a song welled forth from my joyous heart,
As waters gush from a long-sealed spring
  When the chains of winter are rent apart.
" I 'm coming, I 'm coming, my dove, my dear ;
  In the heaven of thy arms, my own sweet wife,
I 'll usher the birth of the glad new year ;
  I 'm coming, I 'm coming, my love, my life ! ''

       .   .   .   .   .   .

Hark ! the clang of the changing sentry's steel ;
  Awaken, O fool, from thy blissful bed ;
On the stony floor of thy dungeon kneel,
  And hug thy chain, for the dream is fled.

HOW OFT A SENTRY SAD AND LONE.

HOW oft, a sentry sad and lone,
  The starry midnight host I've counted,
As up the eastern horizon
  Into the sky they slowly mounted.

Two still seemed missing from their place,
  The brightest of the heavenly number;
But now I find them in thy face,
  Nightly they beam upon my slumber.

FROM COPLAS OF AN ANDALUSIAN
SOLDIER.

IF daring deeds might win thy vows,
   At nothing would I falter ;
I 'd dare thy father's beetling brows,
   Or those of grim Gibraltar.

I 'll seek the thickest of the strife,
   And lofty deeds of glory ;
My girl shall be a General's wife,
   Or mourn a lover gory.

Light batteries on the fatal field,
   Their countless victims strewing,
Are the bright eyes to which I yield
   For quarter meekly suing.

Thy lips are silken banners, and
   Beneath their crimson lustre,
In gleaming lines the soldiers stand,
   Two ranks prepared for muster.

The girl that jilts a veteran bold
   To marry a clodhopper,
Would throw away the finest gold
   To pick up worthless copper.

FROM THE SAME.

THE conscripts march, O cruel theft,
   While those that are rejected,
The crooked and the lame, are left
   To comfort maids dejected.

If swift promotion you would gain,
   Yet shrink from war and slaughter,
The path is old and very plain—
   Marry the General's daughter.

THE GLORY OF A SPANISH DRAGOON.

FROM THE SAME.

M Y little Pepita
   Will be jealous I know,
For I promised to meet her,
   But how can I go ?
I come off of guard,
   And go on police ;
My sergeant 's a hard
   One, and gives me no peace.
There 's the devil to pay
   At fatigue duty too ;
Every hour of the day
   There is something to do.
A soldier at work,
   What a pitiful sight !
I 'd desert to the Turk
   In the very next fight,
But his way of baptizing
   You all will agree,
Is quite too surprising,
   It would never suit me.

But my sergeant is worse
  Than a Turk or a Jew,
He finds something to curse
  At, whatever I do.
At every roll-call,
  If I 'm not upon time,
Drill, stables, and all,
  He counts it a crime ;
He laughs at my story,
  In the guard-house I 'm thrown,—
And this is the glory
  Of a Spanish dragoon.
    10

WRITTEN FOR A REUNION OF VETER-
ANS IN THE YEAR 1915.

COMRADES, once more to-night we gather
here,
A dwindling band of graybeards; autumn sere
Pales into winter, Indian summer's glow
Fades from the hills, reluctant still to go;
And Earth itself fades from our sight away,
Like rosy clouds that flit at close of day;
In our hearts too the flame burns low at last,—
An arctic winter closes round us fast.

While the remaining grains, how few, alas !
Of golden sand, pour through the hour-glass,
Fill up, dear friends, your goblets once again,
And warm the pulses in each shrunken vein
With sunshine garnered on some Gallic plain,
Or stolen from the vine-clad hills of Spain.
Here 's to the living absent, comrades they
So gay in camp, so dauntless in the fray,
The lingering remnant of the mighty host
That swept from far Atlanta to the coast.
Since then their prows through every sea have
foamed,
And o'er five continents their feet have roamed,

And plucked the brightest bays in fields afar,
Who glittered brightest in the van of war.
But fast and faster from our sight they fail,
A few belated stragglers feebly hail
Along the banks of Styx the boatman pale.
Where'er they are, once more we pledge them all,
Ere from the thinning ranks we too shall fall.

Lift high the cup, a generous current pour,
Libations to the chosen friends of yore,
Who wander on the dim Plutonian shore.
A mist arises from the wine-stained ground,
And lo, what phantom faces gather round !
Like storm-blown wreaths they flit—e'en so must
    we
Soon pass like vapors blown across the sea.

Now draw together, fling apart the doors
Of wit and fancy, open up the stores
Of feeling that have been repressed so long ;
Waken the voice of melody and song,
These fleeting moments sweetly to prolong,
And kindling up once more the altar fire,
Let the last embers all in flame expire.

TWENTY-FIVE SONNETS

TO ———

DEAR lady, doth the singer's voice in thee
   Awake an answering chord ? if not so, be
Barren the song and all devoid of worth,
Save to awaken idle scorn and mirth ;
Thy soul, self-poised in cold tranquillity,
Will smile to think how foolish some may be.
But if thy bosom swell with tender sighs,
If the deep fountains of thy soul are stirred,
Meeting some dear but unexpected word ;
If, answering mine, responsive pulses rise,
And thy lips tremble to the happy eyes
Suffused with pleasure at the glad surprise
Of verses all too cold for thy completeness,
   Know thy own heart hath lent them all their
      sweetness.

POESY.

BEFORE the human hand a stylus held,
Ere papyrus' or parchment's mute appeal,
Sweet songs were sung whose echoes charm us
    still ;
From dying lips undying music welled.
Wedded to strains from chosen souls that swelled,
Were rescued from oblivion's clammy seal,
Fantastic legend, laws of commonweal,
Heroic deeds in days of hoary eld.

Muse of the lyre and harp, till latest day
Thy voice shall bear along the shores of Time,
While kingdoms crumble, and while tongues de-
    cay,
The numbers of the ancient bards sublime.
Still thy anointed favorites hold their sway,
'Mid falling stars, and gods that pass away.

THE ROSE.

THE flushing wave bloomed into wondrous
flower,
And rosy light burst forth unknown till then,
When Aphrodite dawned on gods and men.
Thy birth, O Rose, was in that mystic hour.
Transcendent Rose, pride of the Paphian bower,
And sweet consoler of the thorny glen,
What virgin charms thy blush illumines when
Upon the virgin heart Love seals his power.

Fair as the lily was the Rose's breast ;
But when the generous vine upon it bled,
Swift blushes o'er its swelling beauties spread
Till every leaf the tender flame confessed,
While from thy wakened heart, O queenly Rose,
Ambrosial incense on the air arose.

TO A FAIR SANTA BARBARAN.

WHY blooms the fairest flower 'neath rosy
skies,
Where all is bloom and fragrance? why unfold
There, where the nectar that its petals hold
Among the orange groves neglected lies,
And all its perfume all unheeded dies!
    And thou, dear maid, with wealth of love un-
    told,
    More precious far than mines of gems and gold,
Why linger 'mid these cloyed and listless eyes?

O with thy voice, and smile ineffable,
    And eyes so meet for sympathetic tears,
    Seek some sad land oppressed by grief and
    fears,
A bright consoling angel there to dwell;
Fly, ere thy robes are wet with honey dew,
And thy own sweetness cloys thee through and
    through.

LA DIVA.

A SEA of faces ripple round her where,
   As on a sunny isle, the Diva glows
Behind the footlights like a full-blown rose ;
A hush expectant fills the brooding air.

But hist, O hist ! what dying cygnet there?
   How bubbling from her alabaster throat
   Pours forth the wave of every passion's note—
Hope, fear, love's ecstasy, and blank despair?

A moment's silence ere the plaudits rise,
   Till like a storm they beat the trembling walls,
And white hands plash like wave-crests to the
      skies.
   Alas ! 't is o'er, the jealous curtain falls ;
And as the tumult of our rapture dies,
A misty curtain veils our happy eyes.

TO A HAPPY LOVER.

FLAUNT not before the world thy happy love,
  Like the poor fatuous one whose pleasure
    lies
Not in Love's glance, but in the envious eyes
Of other fools ; deep in the myrtle grove
Seek some untrodden way, shadowed above ;
  There, if Love will, his unknown harmonies,
  His inmost heart and core, his tears and sighs,
And unimagined mysteries thou mayest prove.

But if thou find his choicest fruits and flowers,
  Guard them from eyes profane with jealous
    care ;
  Love, proud but tender, brooks no sign-board
    there,
Pointing the pathway to his sacred bowers ;
Himself the entrance, hidden and o'ergrown,
Unto his chosen favorites will make known.

METEMPSYCHOSIS.

I.

I WAS a huntsman in my youth, and knew
Each bird and beast that haunts the forest
  tall,
Or wings the air, hard by the water-fall.
Over the plain and up the mountain blue
My twanging bow was heard, my arrows flew.
  My bowstring now is rent, my arrows all
  Like spears that from the withered pine-cones
    fall,
Have from my shrunken quiver vanished too.
Yet sometimes o'er me steals the olden mood,
  And wandering in the forest deep and dark,
  I greet each old familiar tree and mark,
Each spot whereon the lovely quarry stood,
While faintly through my withered veins once
  more
Leaps the triumphant thrill I knew of yore.

II.

I shot an arrow through the wood one day
  In idle sport, and following where it led,
  I found a doe that I had raised and fed,

Stricken, and bleeding fast her life away,
Her tender fawn transfixed beside her lay ;
  One random shaft two happy lives had sped.
  The dry leaves rustled to my startled tread,
And filled my fluttering heart with strange
    dismay ;
For gazing in those failing eyes my soul
  Found there another soul, its very twin ;
  Unseen for years, but bowered deep within
The heart's alcove,—oh, lost beyond control !
Those murdered eyes still gaze as from a glass
Framed in with bloody leaves and trampled grass.

THREE SONNETS IN MEMORIAM.

I.

DESPAIR—THE ABYSS.

O DREAD abyss, narrow, but dark and deep,
Still baffling all that men may do or dare
To read the secrets of thy jealous care,
The mystery that thy shuddering caverns keep,
Over thy cruel mouth the earth I heap,
Hiding my treasure like a miser there.
My hollow doubting voice I lift in prayer ;
With ghastly lips I say : " ' 'T is but a sleep,
And I shall find my loved one freed from sorrow,
Glowing with love, and youth ineffable."
O fool, the only sure thing thou canst borrow
From coming years is death, thou knowest well.
Yet even this is gain ; then hail each morrow
That brings thee nearer to the self-same cell.

II.

QUESTIONING.

Beneath the leafless trees alone I stand,
Where we two stood in June. O loved one, where
Are now the radiant hopes that filled the air,
Circling around us swiftly like a band

Of smiling sisters, clasping hand in hand ?
　Dearer to me than all their visions fair
　This chill December night, so thou wert there.
And hast thou sought with them some better land ?

Would heaven be darkened for one form the less
　From the bright throng who in His love rejoice ?
　From the celestial choir could not one voice,
Sweeter than all the rest, be spared to bless
My solitude ?　Say, dost thou sleep alone,
Voiceless, beneath the unrelenting stone ?

III.

CONSOLATION.

Alone ?　Ah, no : beneath the earth's fair crust
　Assemble all the beautiful and good
　Whose memory transfigures womanhood ;
And kingly men are there, the brave, the just ;
How sweet to mingle with that sacred dust !
　Standing to-night where we so oft have stood,
　Their fragrance fills the silent solitude—
Sweet flowers of human love and hope and trust.

Where'er thou art, O sister of my soul,
　Treading with gleaming feet the streets of gold,
　Or softly mingling with the forest mold,
Swift years shall bear me to the self-same goal,
Our radiant heads in the same aureole,
　Or the same flower-roots thrill our ashes cold.

IN MEMORY OF D. G. R.

BATHED in the morning sunlight thou didst
stand,
The sisters nine in homage gathered round,
Son of Apollo, with his laurels crowned,
His lyre of lyres trembling in thy hand.
The brush and chisel at thy high command
Enchantment wrought, but sweeter far resounds
The music of thy verse, the soulful sounds
Flung from thy pen as from a magic wand.

Had all thy wondrous powers to song been given,
What floods of melody had filled the air—
Eros' and Psyche's voices mingling there.
Alas! the wine is spilled, the lyre is riven,
Stern Albion's son, thy soft Italian name
Lives only in the Pantheon of Fame.

IN MEMORY OF JOHN BROWN OF OSSA-
WATTOMIE.

INSCRIBED TO JOHN J. INGALLS.

I.

A CLOUD for years o'erhung the border-land,
  Black, ominous, wherein were dimly seen
Soul-terrifying shapes of beasts unclean,
And men uncleaner still, a hideous band,
Loathsome as reptiles from the slimy strand
  Of vanished seas, in ages pliocene.
  Prophets the portent read with vision keen,
But lying seers cried " Peace," throughout the
    land,
'T is but a cloud-bank changing with the wind,
  And craven hearts draw their own pictures there,
And traitors sneered, and from the pulpit whined
Sleek hypocrites, blind leaders of the blind,
  Buyers of souls, who gathered gold with care,
  With gnashing and blaspheming filled the air.

II.

A soul flamed forth like a titanic brand,
  Or fiery meteor through the murky sky,
  Thrilled by electric arrows from on high ;
And by swift wings of unseen seraphs fanned
The baleful clouds dispersed, as though a hand
  Omnipotent had swept the firmament
  And from its face the darkening veil had rent.
Vague shapes of fear, as by enchanter's wand,
Were changed to forms substantial, and arose
  The Nation's foes, implacable and fierce.
  The canting knave, who chapter gave and verse
To justify the trade in human woes,
Slunk with his broad phylacteries away,
And strong men armed them for the deadly fray.

III.

True greatness is the greatest in defeat.
  A laurel wreath entwined about that head
  Had but obscured the glory that it shed.
Unshaken in his high prophetic seat,
Beyond all crowns of vict'ry grand and great
  In happier days, as when, illusions fled,
  His fierce foes found him lying 'mid his dead,
Alike his spirit soared secure from Fate.

So, when the charging battle standards meet,
　Gold fringe and silken fold are plucked away
　As by the myriad beaks of birds of prey,
Still on the staff, high in his ancient seat,
The brazen eagle sits, serene, the same,
Pride of the legions o'er the battle's flame.

OUR LOST ONES.

"Hélas ! dans le cercueil ils tombent en poussière
Moins vite qu'en nos cœurs."
—HUGO.

BRETHREN and sisters all, what do we here,
With song and laughter, while around us
stand,
With dumb reproachful gaze, a shadowy band,
The mournful shades of all our lost ones dear?
O conquering power of the eternal years !
How swiftly fade away on every hand
Their memories throughout the joyous land,
For whom we thought to shed eternal tears.

Smiling above them wave the flowers and grass,
Where cold and still those cherished forms are
strown,
Thickly as grain in the deep furrows sown,
Or sheaves in fields where merry reapers pass.
To dust they wither in our hearts, alas !
More swiftly than beneath the cruel stone.

THE OCEAN OF THE PAST.

M Y wistful eyes still sweep thy sullen breast,
   Dead sea, whose waves, once, following
      stroke on stroke,
Have swallowed mast and sail and hull of oak.
Now all thy cruel billows are at rest ;
Hushed is thy roar, and stilled each raging crest ;
   No phantom from thy mists may I evoke,
   No more my prow or sail the waves provoke,
Where sleeps my happy island of the blest.

Lo, while I gaze, like the responsive swell
   Of some great yearning heart, the billows rise,
   Till, in wild tumult leaping to the skies,
They toss the beauteous wrecks I loved so well,
   Resistless through the rending barriers roll
   And sob through all the caverns of my soul.

EVIL DAYS.

O YOUTH, O Hope, O Love, all phantoms
vain !
Ye lured me long with promise false as sweet,
But now your flight outstrips my faltering feet.
Dear traitors, will ye ne'er return again ?
Love lingered last, but all have been too fleet.
 Now sinks the light of day in tears and pain,
 The glories of the night unheeded wane :
Summer is winter, truth is but deceit.

Shall I not find upon some vernal day,
 Fruition for the buds that blighted here ?
The golden hours of youth I cast away,
 How I would hold those wasted treasures dear !
Still through the lonely chambers of my brain
No more, no more, echoes the sad refrain.

ENVY AND SLANDER.

TO N. A. M.

ENVY is deathless, though the envious die,
   And shafts of slander, hissing through the
      dark,
Have ever loved, like death, a shining mark.
Then do not think those shafts could pass thee by.

Thy conscious worth, and purpose pure and high
   Cannot defend from little curs that bark ;
   No wall, high as the flight of morning lark,
Can top the poisoned arrows as they fly.

Rise o'er the herd in feeling, thought, or deed,
   And feel the bitter sting of Envy's tongue ;
   Rise higher yet, and thus confound the throng,—
Only a respite brief thy soul may read.
Success, e'en more than merit, is a crime
To tongues as tireless as the feet of Time.

TRUE FREEDOM.

TO J. F. F.

HE is not truly free who fears to speak
   The burning words that flame from heart
      to tongue,
When in the presence of a hoary wrong,
E'en though upheld by gown and surplice sleek,
And hears unheeded the oppressed and weak.
   Nor friendship from the great, the rich, the
      strong,
   Nor grateful plaudits from the servile throng,
The free-born spirit must expect or seek.

Think not that power and place will come to
      thee—
   Sooner some sordid soul the race will win ;
   E'en in the days of Cid and Paladin,
And glorious days of Arthur's chivalry,
The golden spurs by cravens oft were won,
While hearts as brave as Arthur's died unknown.

"SOCIETY."

DEAR, simple friend, and did you think to find
     Aught but hypocrisy and fair smooth lies
In this charmed circle, that would ostracize
All for a pair of gloves the most refined,
The noblest type of man or womankind?
     A set whose aspirations never rise
     Above the triumphs wealth and fashion buys;
Who ape the opinions with devotion blind,
The coats and gowns, of royal debauchees
And their bold paramours from over seas.
     How hope a noble womanhood to gain
Nourished upon such stifling airs as these.
     Fashion forbids to rise above a plane
     That dudes and lah-de-dahs can just attain.

THE STAGNANT POOL.

STOOPING beside a stagnant pool to drink
    I saw a woman, weary and forlorn,
    With hair unkempt, and garments stained and
        torn ;
All grace of womanhood was fled, no link
Remained of happier days ; along the brink
    Swept by a stately dame with words of scorn ;
    " Though I had thirsted since the early morn,
Before my feet in that foul wave should sink
My willing lips should press the cup of death."
    O scornful dame ! before the night was black,
    Lo ! I beheld thy swift feet speeding back,
With robes dishevelled and with gasping breath,
In this same wave thy parching lips to cool,
As eagerly as 't were a mountain pool.

THE MAN WITH THE MUCK-RAKE.

A N old and well-known allegory reading,
I found a quaint and curious picture there,
Of one who gathered straws and dirt with care,
The golden crown above his head unheeding.
Science to-day, than avarice more misleading,
Hath slain our father's faith and hope and
prayer ;
We rake the seas, and sweep the earth and air
To find new theories for our own impeding.

And some for tinsel toys of social glory,
And Church and State, toil through the grovel-
ling years.
How can we hear the music of the spheres,
Clutching the muck-rakes of the allegory ?
Our blunted senses only can discern
The paltry baubles over which we yearn.

IMMORTALITY.

M Y vision floats far down the milky-way,
   A shining track across a shoreless sea
As deep and boundless as eternity.
Suns sail in myriads there, and comets stray,
Youthful, while hoary ages roll away.
   O fleeting life, the stars that shine on me
   Smiled just the same when star-lit Galilee
Beneath the Saviour's feet in slumber lay.

What countless swarms of man's ephemeral race
   Live, love, and die, while ye sail coldly on !
   Yet they shall rise, the teeming millions gone,
And gaze unmoved, while from their ancient
      place
The morning stars like baleful meteors fleet,
And while the heavens melt with fervent heat.

TO A YOUNG ARTIST.

THE matchless artists of the olden time
   Knew naught of critic's jargon ; to their toil
   Bending as one that digs a stony soil,
Sparing nor bloom of youth nor manhood's
      prime,
They caught and fixed their floating dreams sub-
      lime.
   So must we shun all vain polemic broil,
   Nor vex our souls with theories' turmoil
If to ideal heights we fain would climb.

Our vintage time is speeding fast away,
   The morning faileth ; then with double will,
   In spite of noonday glare or evening chill,
Gather the glowing clusters while we may.
So may our failing eyes see some faint beams
Shed o'er our work from our supernal dreams.

THE END.

176

www.ingramcontent.com/pod-product-compliance
Lightning Source LLC
Chambersburg PA
CBHW022358020726

47500CB00002B/328